A hologram of the area of space along the front line appeared in front of Benny and Gina.

Benny was surprised at how many thousands of small green dots, which represented Seeder ships, appeared around *Star Mist*'s position in space.

On the left were the alien occupied galaxies, on the right were the galaxies they were trying to protect from the alien ships.

"*Star Mist*, now add in the alien ships," Angie said.

The entire hologram almost turned completely red with dots representing alien ships.

Angie gasped.

Gina clamped down on Benny's hand.

Benny said simply, "Shit."

It was a massive sea of millions and millions of alien ships. And a lot of the red dots were into the galaxies behind the front line.

Benny felt sick.

"We are so screwed," Gage said.

Benny could only agree with that.

STAR RAIN

ALSO BY DEAN WESLEY SMITH

ALSO BY DEAN WESLEY SMITH

STAR RAIN

A SEEDERS UNIVERSE NOVEL

DEAN WESLEY SMITH

wmg
PUBLISHING

Star Rain

Copyright © 2022 by Dean Wesley Smith

Published in a different form in *Smith's Monthly #26*, November, 2015

Published by WMG Publishing

Cover and Layout copyright © 2022 by WMG Publishing

Cover design by Allyson Longueira/WMG Publishing

Cover art copyright © Philcold | Dreamstime

ISBN-13: 978-1-56146-731-0

ISBN-10: 1-56146-731-6

For Kris

SECTION ONE

THE FIGHT IS LOST

PROLOGUE

TWENTY-SEVEN YEARS BEFORE THE
DISCOVERY OF THE ALIENS...

The last three years had gone faster than Chairman Evan West had expected. Around him on the command center of the *Rescue One*, the fifteen members of his main crew were all standing ready at their stations on the three levels, all scanning ahead as much as they could.

He knew that through the entire ship the thirty thousand people on board were also watching intently.

West was a tall, thin man with bright green eyes, balding head, and wide shoulders. People said he had a smile that made him a lot of friends and he liked to laugh and have fun.

Lately he hadn't smiled much.

The air was tense in the large room around him, but professional. The large screen that filled the tall wall in front of them only showed the quickly approaching front edge of the small galaxy they were calling Destination. The galaxy had a number, but no one called it by that anymore.

West stood beside his large chairman's chair, watching not only his instruments, but those of his second and third in command at their stations on either side of him.

Nothing.

Just nothing out of the ordinary at all.

They were on a mission to find out what had happened to the *Dreaming Large,* one of the huge Seeder mother ships. It had vanished in the small galaxy they were now approaching.

That had been four years ago, a short time for a Seeder, but a very long time for a major mother ship to vanish completely.

Mother ships were the size of large moons and built to look like a giant bird in flight. A mother ship could hold a few thousand smaller ships and upward of a million or more people. It was from the mother ships that Seeders spread humanity from one galaxy to another, always moving forward.

Chairman West had been a seeder now for three thousand years and had seen many galaxies along the way. And he had helped in birthing more billions of human societies than he wanted to even try to imagine.

He loved his job.

He didn't much like this mission.

His wife and best friend, Tammy, had been on the *Dreaming Large* when it vanished. He missed their nightly routines of telling each other their days through a trans-tunnel link, even when they had been apart for years. He loved her and always had loved her. They had been a team for centuries.

And he missed her now more than he wanted to ever admit.

Their plan had been for him to finish up the last part of a seeding mission in the previous galaxy and then his ship and a dozen other front-line ships with him would catch up with the *Dreaming Large*. He liked working the front edge of the seeding as he always did after the terraforming was finished.

He had worried for the three years it took them at full trans-tunnel speed to get here and he had missed Tammy every moment of it. He had no idea what they were going to find. No one had an idea, even though the speculation was rampart.

How could a major Seeder mother ship simply vanish?

Without a word of notice, the two chairmen who jointly ran the mother ship had stopped reporting in to Chairman Ray.

When that had happened, Chairman Ray had contacted him and the idea of *Rescue One* was born.

There were twenty-two mother ships now, built over centuries, with more being built all the time. The *Dreaming Large* was the first to vanish.

Tammy had been one of the head botanists on *Dreaming Large*. She had loved her job, just as he loved his.

The *Rescue One* had been built especially for this mission.

Unlike most Seeders' ships, the *Rescue One* had a full military contingent and four warships on board, commanded by West's best friend, Ben Cline. Seeders, by their very mission and scouting ahead, never had much need for military until some of the growing new human cultures hit their early space age stage. So to even put together a military fleet, Cline had scrounged through some more advanced human cultures recently seeded for ships and enough new Seeders to man the ships.

It had taken Cline as long to put his force together as it had to build the *Rescue One*.

The *Rescue One* had been built in preparation for almost anything they might find. It also had in its huge hangar twenty of the Seeders' fastest scout ships, all crewed with upward of twenty thousand people each and ready to go.

And it had room, if necessary, for a hundred thousand survivors, a fraction of the humans who had been on the *Dreaming Large* when it vanished.

Now, finally, after the year of building and three years of travel at the fastest trans-tunnel speeds any Seeder ship could go, they were almost there.

"Anything?" West asked, breaking the silence on the large command center and glancing around the three levels at his first shift crew.

All of them shook their heads.

"Full stop at scouting distance from the edge of Destination," he ordered.

"We'll be at full stop in one minute," Korgan said.

Korgan was his second in command and had been chairman of his own scout ship before volunteering to go on this mission. He had family, a son and a daughter, on the *Dreaming Large*.

In fact, a good third of the crew of the *Rescue One* had family or some personal connection to crew on the *Dreaming Large*.

That made this crew very, very motivated to find the lost mother ship.

"Dropping out of trans-warp now," Korgan said, his voice seeming to almost echo in the silence of the large bridge.

"Full scans," West said.

Then he motioned to Korgan to have the crews of the scout ships stand ready and be scanning as well.

West moved over and stood beside his command chair. He couldn't make himself sit in the chair until they knew what had happened to *Dreaming Large*. But from where he stood, he could see all the data streaming in.

Destination was a small spiral galaxy on the scheme of things, with about 80 billion stars of all standard sizes. It showed no unusual areas at all.

And not a sign of the *Dreaming Large*.

Nothing.

The huge mother ship had just vanished.

West left his chairman's chair after a few minutes and walked slowly around to all the stations on his bridge, not so much for information, but to give everyone some time and let himself relax a little.

He had been preparing for this moment for four years. Rushing anything now might lead to even more problems.

Finally, after the longest half hour he had ever spent in the command center, he broke the intense silence.

"Let's have some reports," he said. "So everyone can be together on this. And broadcast these reports to the entire ship please."

Korgan nodded for West to go ahead.

"Anything unusual at all about Destination?"

Three stations reported in that there was nothing unusual. Then Korgan added. "What we are reading matches exactly the last reports of the scout ships two hundred years before the *Dreaming Large* arrived here."

West nodded. "Any signs of alien or human habitation?"

Six reports came in quickly, one after another, cutting the small galaxy down into six quadrants, just as it would have been seeded.

Nothing.

No alien life, no human life, no remains of any ship anywhere.

As with most galaxies, this one was empty. And if it had an alien race at any level anywhere in the galaxy, the entire galaxy would have just been left alone and the *Dreaming Large* would have gone on to the next empty galaxy.

Not one sign that the *Dreaming Large* had even started terraforming the Goldilocks zone planets around yellow stars. Whatever had happened, it had happened before the *Dreaming Large* entered Destination.

"More information as we have it," West said, signaling to Korgan to cut the communication to the entire ship.

West did one more walk around the bridge, looking at details on a few reports, but finding nothing different at all.

Finally, he went down to stand near his station.

"*Rescue One*," he said, "please put on the screen a two-dimensional representation of the galaxies closest to Destination. Limit the galaxies to a one-year travel time for the *Dreaming Large* from this point."

Thirty-one galaxies came up, represented as dots. There were a couple clusters and ten galaxies seemed to have formed a group. Over the last three years he had stared at this very map more than he wanted to admit.

But he knew that the *Dreaming Large* would not have gone to any of those other galaxies without reporting in. And with Destination being an empty galaxy, perfect for seeding, there would have been no reason to move on.

This was exactly what he had feared. What Chairman Ray had also feared.

"Now, *Rescue One*," West said to his ship, "please add into the scanning equipment the ability to see pockets of empty space."

Everyone on the bridge crew just stopped and looked at him like he had lost a marble or two.

Almost no one had heard of empty space. He hadn't either until this mission started.

West had been briefed by Chairman Ray and his wife, Chairman Tacita, on the very reality of empty space, or void space as it was sometimes called.

Basically, empty space was a very small bubble in space, often not more than the size of a standard solar system, where space was completely empty and time and the rules of physics did not apply for some reason inside it.

Over the centuries, Seeder ships had just vanished when they ran into a bubble of empty space.

And they would often emerge thousands, if not hundreds of thousands of years later having only spent less than a ship-board few hours in empty space.

Chairman Ray had warned West that if there were no logical reasons for *Dreaming Large* to have vanished, no signs of

9

any debris, or any human survivors, then West was to look for empty space pockets.

The scientists on some of the more advanced Seeder ships had developed a program to show complete emptiness, something normal space did not have.

It had taken the scientists three years of frantic work to finally develop and test the long-range scanning program.

And if this worked, every Seeder ship would get the program as an update and hopefully no more ships would be lost to centuries in an empty space bubble.

For the year that the scanning program had been uploaded to *Rescue One*, the scientists had continued to make adjustments and sent them along. West had told no one about any of it.

"Loaded," *Rescue One* said.

"Display on the screen as dots the empty space areas within four galaxies radius of this location," West said.

Then red dots appeared. Only about eight total in that much space, but one was seemingly right where they were.

They were within brushing distance of the edge of an empty space bubble.

"Shit!' West said. "Back us away from the edge of that thing to a distance of two light years."

West couldn't believe that they had almost vanished right into empty space as well.

That had been far, far too close.

"We're back away from it," Korgan reported a few long moments later. "What exactly is empty space?"

"That's where the *Dreaming Large* is trapped," West said.

The big mother ship had to be right here very close to them, only stuck in a bubble of no time and space. And the mother ship might not emerge for a hundred thousand years.

All West could see in his mind was the smiling face of his wife.

Somehow, they had to rescue the big ship, even though, more than likely, no one on the big ship even knew anything was wrong yet.

But he and *Rescue One* and its crew had to pull off the impossible and get *Dreaming Large* out of there.

Somehow.

Over the next five years, the *Rescue One* went from a military-based rescue operation to a full-fledged science ship. West had remained as chairman on request, a request that Chairman Ray had gladly granted.

And Chairman Ray had put West in charge of the overall mission. All ships' chairmen in the area reported to him.

Entire parts of *Rescue One* were being reconfigured into research labs to study the empty space bubble holding the *Dreaming Large* mother ship.

Admiral Cline had taken all his military ships and headed back to help out at the last seeded galaxy with upcoming wars between developing human planets.

The fleet of scout ships they had brought with them all scattered out to do what they do, scout ahead, map galaxies and spot trouble galaxies that had the occasional growing alien race.

Almost every day another science ship arrived at *Rescue One* and took a location either in space near *Rescue One* or on one of the large decks where the military ships and scout ships had once been housed.

Almost fifty smaller science ships had now surrounded the small bubble of empty space, studying it, trying to see inside it.

Every Seeder's ship now had the scanning ability to see and avoid empty space bubbles, something that West had no doubt would save ships from losing thousands and thousands of years.

Now they just had to figure out a way to get the *Dreaming Large* out of there in under a few thousand years.

Every day Chairman West had a meeting with the four top science advisors to get reports on any progress. They usually met for breakfast in his own kitchen in his apartment, taking turns cooking and cleaning and talking about the problem.

All four were chairmen of their own major science ships.

It was right before one meeting that West came up with an idea. He had been sitting at his kitchen counter, staring at a surface rendering of the patterns on the border of the empty space and he suddenly saw it a different way.

They had been working to find a way to shield themselves from the effects of the empty space, go in and shield *Dreaming Large* as well. What would happen if they just drained the empty space out into normal space?

Or better yet, filled empty space with normal space.

In essence, they needed to pop the bubble, leaving the *Dreaming Large* surprised at all the company it suddenly had around it.

The four scientists loved that idea and after the meeting, West contacted Chairman Ray and told him about it to get scientists in numbers of galaxies working on the problem as well.

It took seven more years to find the solution.

Seven very long and frustrating years.

Now West stood in the command center of the *Rescue One* yet again, sixteen years after he had agreed to join this project, ready to try to finally release *Dreaming Large*.

As everyone had been warned, no one on *Dreaming Large* would even realize they had been in trouble. As far as those on board the giant mother ship knew, only a few seconds had transpired since they entered empty space and their trans-tunnel drives had suddenly shut down.

If what *Rescue One* and all the other ships were about to do worked, the hundreds and hundreds of ships that now swarmed the area would suddenly just appear to those on *Dreaming Large*.

If it worked.

And if the forces didn't pull *Dreaming Large* apart.

Chairman Ray and others had said that the giant mother ships were designed to withstand plowing into planets and going right on through. Ray wasn't worried about that at all.

But West was.

They had calculated the trajectory where *Dreaming Large* had entered the empty space bubble and cleared every ship out of the way where it would be headed.

What they were going to try to do was in essence take the pressure of empty space away by opening not just one, but thousands of holes in it all at once. Just as firefighters did to a burning structure under pressure. They opened many outlets instead of just one.

The scientists a few years back had determined exactly what strange gravitational force was holding empty space together like a bubble, allowing a ship to enter and leave, yet holding the space together.

And once they had determined that force, they knew how to puncture the force to not so much let empty space out, but to let regular space and time flood in.

The entire bubble should, the scientists had told West, just vanish as if it had never existed.

West could only hope.

"Report status," West said to all the ships around the bubble ready to send a hundred probes each to open up holes.

A moment later Korgan looked up at him and nodded. "All eighty ships report green, Chairman."

West nodded, staring at the big screen in front of him showing nothing but empty space.

"Mission go," West said.

West knew that once he said that, a computer program from *Rescue One* would launch all probes at the exact same moment from all ships.

West had been told that the probes would have a small charge when they hit the membrane, so it would look like eight thousand tiny lights flashing at the same time in a sphere shape in open space.

"Five seconds," Korgan said.

Intense, heavy silence filled the bridge of the ship.

West had no doubt not one word was being said anywhere in the large fleet of ships surrounding the empty space bubble.

West could not for a second take his gaze away from the massive screen in front of him.

Suddenly, there was a white flash of light from what looked like the surface of a sphere.

Then a moment later, the massive mother ship *Dreaming Large* appeared.

Cheering erupted around the bridge.

West just stood there grinning, staring at the screen, knowing that finally, after sixteen years, he would finally get to see his wife's face again. And maybe a little later actually hug her and kiss her.

After a moment, Korgan, a smile almost splitting his face, turned to West. "I have the two chairmen of the *Dreaming Large* asking just what the hell is going on."

West just smiled right back at Korgan. "Tell them to contact Chairman Ray and let him explain."

Then, for seemingly the first time in sixteen years, he went and sat down in his chairman's chair.

And then on a private channel he said to *Rescue One*, "Please contact my wife on *Dreaming Large* and put her through to my personal screen here."

"I will be glad to, Chairman," *Rescue One* said.

"Thank you," he said.

And then, for the first time in sixteen years, he took a deep breath and relaxed.

CHAPTER 1
SIXTY-THREE YEARS AFTER THE RESCUE
OF THE DREAMING LARGE

Chairman Benny Slade stood beside Gina Helm, his co-chairman of the Seeder mother ship *Star Rain*, in their massive command center, watching the newest reports come in on the big wall-sized screen from their sector of space.

Beside them their molded joint command chair dominated the large room, but neither of them felt like sitting in it at the moment.

There were twenty others at stations in the command center behind them and not a person was saying a word. The room was the size of a banquet room and three levels, with one wall filled with a massive screen.

Benny had on his normal jeans and dress shirt with the sleeves rolled up. He worked out and ran every day and kept his dark hair military short. He loved this job more than anything he could have ever imagined. But sometimes, on days like today, he would rather be doing just about anything else.

Gina was as tall as his six-foot height, had black hair, and was in as good shape physically as he was. She had on a long-sleeve white blouse, jeans, and tennis shoes. She always kept her long black hair pulled back and tied.

Benny loved Gina more than he could ever imagine loving another human being, and now, after thirty plus years together, couldn't imagine not having her at his side.

"So, what do you think," Gina asked softly, staring at the last reports flowing over the big screen. Everyone in the command center could see the data and no one was saying a word. Tomb-like silence, never a good thing as far as Benny was concerned.

"We're losing this goddamned fight," Benny said.

Gina only nodded.

As more and more scout ships were put out to find alien galaxies, and as the scout ships found the galaxies, many of them just teeming with alien planets, the more it became clear the impossibility of the fight they faced.

Benny glanced around at their command crew as they worked at their stations, quietly, making sure everything on the massive mother ship was running smoothly and clearly not wanting to acknowledge what Benny had just said.

Their ship, *Star Rain*, was shaped like a large bird gliding through space, but it was larger than most moons and functioned more like a flying city than anything else. And it was all controlled by *Star Rain* and the team in this command center.

And Benny knew that all of the team behind him were basically looking at the same data he and Gina were staring at on the big screen.

And he had no doubt all of them were coming to the same damn conclusion he and Gina were facing.

They were losing.

Every one of the over one million people on the *Star Rain* knew it.

No one was talking about giving up or retreating, but unless a miracle occurred, they were not going to be able to contain the aliens.

But they had no real choice if all human-settled galaxies were going to survive. They had to stop this plague of rat-like aliens somehow.

But damned if any of them knew how.

Gina took his hand and squeezed it. They had been together now ever since he had set up the Empire State Building in his hometown of New York City to house survivors from a planet-wide disaster.

She had been a Seeder and assigned to help him. After they had met, he had become a Seeder as well and together they had stayed on his home planet to help in the recovery and rebuilding.

Three long years they worked on the surface, including moving to Portland, one of the new centers of the recovering civilization. That task has seemed impossible as well.

And then one day, seemingly out of the blue, they had been offered this job to be joint chairmen of a massive million-person Seeder mother ship.

It seemed he and Gina had great Seeder genes or some such

thing. Benny had never completely understood that and honestly had never gotten around to asking or looking it up. It didn't matter, they took the job and now stood here.

Three mother ships had been sent to investigate an alien culture, only to find out the alien culture was manmade. The aliens, as everyone just called them, looked like rats and were no smarter than rats, actually, and thanks to the stupidity of their creators, the aliens were spreading faster from galaxy to galaxy than could be stopped.

Benny hated rats. He had right from the start in New York.

Now they had been fighting this fight against these alien rats for sixteen years.

And Benny was feeling more frustrated by the day.

"Chairmen Ray and Tacita are asking for you presence on the *Star Mist,*" *Star Rain* reported.

Star Rain, their wonderful ship, had an intelligence that was more like their friend to Gina and him than a huge ship. But without *Star Rain,* nothing in this moon-sized ship would work.

Gina laughed. "Wonder if this is more bad news."

Benny smiled at her and then pointed to the big screen. "More bad news? I thought I was the fatalistic one around here."

"Oh, yeah, I forgot," she said, smiling at him and talking in her pretend voice. "Let's go hear the great news they bring that will pull our asses out of this fire and save the day."

"That's better," he said, laughing.

It sure had seemed over the years, since this fight had started, that more bad news had come than good. The aliens had expanded from their first world in three major directions and had been expanding for a couple hundred thousand years now.

The human idiots who designed and genetically built the aliens were an old group who had split away from the Seeders millions of years before. They called themselves The Creators. They believed in being able to create intelligent life from alien structures.

Now they were also fighting against their own creations. No one on a Seeder ship had even talked with them.

And a second ancient fleet of humans calling themselves The Exterminators had followed The Creators and were working now as well to clean up this mess.

So now three fleets of humans were attacking this problem and none of them talking to the other. Benny agreed that at this point, that was for the best.

The idiot Creators had given the aliens only two major drives. First was to have offspring, litters and litters of them. Second designed-in drive was to build trans-tunnel spaceships from a certain pattern and expand to other planets. What a stupid idea. Benny wanted to just meet the Creators and lift them off the ground and shake them and ask them what the hell they were thinking.

The Creators also forgot to program in the aliens simple things like survival and an ability to learn as they went.

In fact, the aliens were almost as dumb as rats in New York. Actually, Benny had seen smarter rats in New York. Thank heavens no one had given the rats in New York the ability to build spaceships.

The more the aliens had been studied over the sixteen years, the more all of the chairmen had come to the conclusion that this race really wasn't intelligent in any real sense of the word. The aliens were just a programmed higher-form rat-like animal and nothing more.

Programmed to breed, expand by building a simple ship, and destroy anything in its way to build more ships.

Benny had a gut sense the destroying part hadn't been programmed in, but was just part of the nature of the creatures.

Rats.

He flat hated rats.

What was amazing is that the aliens didn't even realize they were in a war with their creators. Awareness and communication between the aliens was basically non-existent.

And they had no weapons. They had never been smart enough to create any.

Just their sheer mass and ability to breed was their weapon. And that was enough.

Now, for sixteen years, every resource humanity in hundreds of galaxies could muster quickly was headed here or had gotten here after being retrofitted with the new trans-tunnel drive.

The ship *Star Mist* was on the first front they had outlined at the beginning. Benny and Gina had taken *Star Rain* to a second front and Carey and Matt had taken *Star Fall* to a third front.

The scientists who had studied the alien transports concluded that the best way to destroy an alien ship was a single, low-intensity weapon into the trans-tunnel drive. The alien ship exploded like a kid's balloon against a cactus.

The idea was to destroy all the ships leaving a galaxy and trap the aliens in one galaxy where they would eventually just turn on each other and die off.

But the aliens had to be contained inside the galaxy and galaxies were damn big things and easy for a tiny ship to escape.

So for sixteen years, Benny didn't want to think about the millions of alien ships they had already destroyed. But as more information flowed and more scouting had been done, it was clear to them all that they were losing the fight.

And they were missing alien ships, letting them through to find new galaxies. With the aliens, all it took was one ship to eventually populate an entire galaxy in just six hundred years.

They bred, as the old saying back in New York was, like rats.

They were rats.

Gina reached over and took Benny's hand as he kept staring at the data pouring across the big screen from the newest scouting missions.

"Let's go find out what Chairmen Ray and Tacita want."

"Almost afraid to," Benny said.

"Yeah, I hear you there," Gina said.

A moment later they had transported two hundred galaxies away to another front of this massive war.

CHAPTER 2

Carey and Matt from the *Star Fall* were already there and a moment later their hosts, Angie and Gage from *Star Mist* appeared.

The conference room on *Star Mist* looked the same as the one on *Star Fall*. The room was filled in the center by a long oak-colored wooden table that had two large, high-backed black leather chairs on each side and two on each end. The ceiling was high enough for holographic images to form over the table. And the light was all indirect and always just perfect. There were always beverages and snacks along the back wall.

Gina liked the room, but not what they talked about in the room all the time.

Carey and Matt were also from Benny's home world and had both survived the disaster that killed most of the planet's population. They had both been from the Portland, Oregon, area. Gina liked them both a lot.

Carey was very short, with long brown hair and skin that looked like it had never seen sun. She had an infectious smile that made people around her laugh.

And yet, at the same time, Carey was intense and a fighter and Gina decided she would never want to tangle with her.

Matt was about the same height as Gina and Benny and his short brown hair always seemed to be blowing in all directions at once. He seemed to mostly just sit and listen, but when he said something, it tended to cut right to the problem.

Carey and Matt sat across the wide table from Benny and Gina.

Ray and Tacita looked as they always looked, a black silk shirt for Ray and pantsuit for Tacita. Ray had long, gray hair going down his back and Tacita kept her black hair starkly short.

They were the oldest Seeders by far and had been the first chairman of a mother ship over four million years ago. That was a number that Gina had a hard time even trying to imagine.

She had no idea how two people could live four million years and not be bored or senile. It seemed the special Seeder gene allowed them to remember better and just live forever, barring accidents.

Ray and Tacita sat in their normal seats at the other end of the table opposite Angie and Gage.

Angie had long black hair she kept pulled back and was tall and thin and clearly in shape. She had also come from Benny's home world. Gage was about the same height as Gina and Benny and had a short, military haircut. He had been in the

Seeders responsible for helping the planet recover and had rescued Angie one day and they had been in love ever since.

Gina liked them both a lot. Solid, very, very competent people.

"I think we are ready," Angie said.

Gina glanced at Ray and Tacita at the other end of the table as they both nodded. Gina had to admit that Ray and Tacita had moved mountains in this fight so far and never seemed to tire bringing fighter crews from the Milky Way.

And in these meetings, Angie could never tell if they were bringing good news or bad news.

"Thank you for the meeting and sorry for the short notice," Ray said.

"We assumed you would want to know this," Tacita said.

None of them said a word, letting Ray go on.

"First, as discussed in the last chairmen's meeting on the original Earth, we have seven more mother ships coming in this direction, all fitted with the new drives. And more are clearing their current tasks, retrofitting their drives and will be starting in this direction as well over the next one hundred years."

Gina just shook her head slightly. Seeders not only thought in very large distances, galaxy-spanning distances, often treating galaxies like way-stops or measuring marks along the way, but they also planned in centuries of time. The fact that this fight had been going on now for so long was only a tiny blip to longer-lived Seeders.

"All mother ships have also retrofitted their bays to build and hold only the military mother ships. By the time they arrive each will have thousands more ships to add to the front lines and they are building more every day."

Gina was very glad to hear that again. She and Benny and everyone at the table knew that information already, but it sure felt good to hear once again that a lot more ships were coming to help in this seemingly hopeless fight.

"And fighters from younger galaxies?" Gage asked.

"We are recruiting and training from everywhere," Ray said. "The entire branch of Seeders who helped new recruits has grown into the largest area of all Seeders in just ten years. And we are scanning a thousand seeded planets a week for Seeder genes in the populations."

Gina nodded. She didn't want to ask how many they were finding. It seemed that Seeder genes were very rare things. But there was no doubt the war effort was clearly gearing up on a scale almost impossible to imagine. That was good news, but not news that would be at the level of an emergency meeting.

"A second update before we give you the reason we asked for this meeting," Ray said. "The last of the transit jump stations will be coming online in two weeks."

"Wonderful," Benny said.

Everyone nodded.

Gina agreed. That was good news because the jump stations were a series of stations spaced just the right distance apart so that any Seeder could jump to this area of the known universe, going from one station to the next. She and Benny could jump vast distances because of their training and special gene. But most Seeders had a range of just about 100,000 light years, about the breadth of the Milky Way Galaxy back home.

So to build a jump station from the Seeder-settled part of the universe to here, there were thousands and thousands of jump stations along the track. Building that had been a massive undertaking and Gina, in the beginning, never thought it would be built in time to help.

She had been wrong, clearly.

And she was damn glad she had been.

That meant far more ships could be built here, near the lines and crews could come to their ships without Ray and Tacita having to jump them.

"The big news we have is that we finally have working the extreme long-range scanner," Tacita said.

Gina about came out of her chair. Sixteen years they had been waiting for a scanner that would spot any alien ship even a hundred thousand light years away.

"The scanner will show all alien and human ships in motion within a two-hundred-thousand light-year radius."

"With your permissions," Ray said, "we would like to give the details on building the scanner to your ships."

"It is designed to also work with boosters to expand the range," Tacita said, "so before the system is turned on completely, we will need for ships to spread boosters around to certain locations along all front lines."

"And to the second and third lines of defense as well," Benny said.

"Exactly," Ray said, nodding.

Gina was excited and she could see that Benny was as well. Now, maybe, just maybe, they could see who they were fighting instead of having to just stumble into them in the dark of space.

"And we hope to set up a wall of monitoring stations between this area of space and human-settled areas," Ray said. "That will take a few hundred years to accomplish, but worth the price and safety. The work has already started."

Gina nodded to that as well, as did everyone else.

"How long until the scanners are fully operational in this area?" Gage asked a moment before Gina could ask the exact same question.

"Two years considering all lines of defenses and the time it will take to build and plant the boosters," Ray said.

"But we can test it on galaxies near your ships as soon as your ships have integrated it into their scanning systems," Tacita said.

Ray nodded. "We suggest we do that first before moving forward."

Gina glanced around at the other five chairmen. All of them were nodding.

She smiled at Benny. This could mean the turning point in this fight since over the last sixteen years, the hardest part was just finding the alien ships between galaxies. They missed so many. It had felt at times as if they were taking cups of water out of a waterfall in hopes of stopping the torrent.

Benny nodded and smiled as well, then turned to Ray and Tacita. "Please work with *Star Fall* to get the new scanning system in place."

"And with *Star Mist*," Angie said and Gage nodded.

"And with *Star Rain*," Carey said.

For the first time in a lot of years, Gina felt hopeful that they might have a chance to win this fight.

Or at least slow the expansion down enough to get the full weight of galaxies full of humanity working on the problem in time.

CHAPTER 3

Benny had been excited since Ray and Tacita brought the long-range scanner with them. It seemed that the two inventors of the new trans-tunnel drive had been challenged by the idea of trying to scan for a tiny dot and energy signature from hundreds of thousands of light years away.

The two inventors had been spending the entire time, sixteen years, on the task. As had thousands of other scientists, but it had been those two who had made the breakthrough by using brand new scanning technology that worked in the trans-tunnel space looking for disruptions.

"The scanning system on all three ships are tested and working," *Star Rain* told them four weeks after the meeting with Ray and Tacita.

Star Rain always spoke to Benny and Gina in a solid, female voice and everyone thought of *Star Rain* as female, even though

Benny doubted an intelligent computer thought in terms of gender.

Now it was time to test the new scanner. Benny felt even more excited. Finally, they were going to be able to see what they were fighting.

Finally, after sixteen years.

Benny wasn't sure he wanted to see. But he had to.

They all did.

He and Gina were in their command chair and linked with the other chairmen on the other two mother ships. As always, in the command chair, they held hands and the heads-up displays flowed past them.

While in the chair, Benny felt at times as if he and Gina were in each other's minds. He loved that.

And he could sense *Star Rain* as well.

"*Star Rain*," Gina asked, "how will we be able to tell the difference between an alien ship and a human ship?"

"Alien ships will be designated by a red dot, Seeder ships designated by a green dot, other human ships from The Creators and The Exterminators designated by blue."

"We are ready," Gina said.

"So are we," Carey said.

Benny could hear the excitement in their voices matching his own.

"How about we scan part of our area first," Gage said. "Since we have been trying to stop them here the longest."

All agreed, since the mother ships were too far apart to even come close to overlapping scans at this point. Benny knew that being able to do that would still be a year or more away and would take a lot of signal boosters being built.

"Do we have any boosters online yet?" Angie asked *Star Mist*.

"There are enough boosters online to cover the thirty closest active alien galaxies to this position along what is being called the front line," *Star Mist* replied to all the chairmen.

Benny liked the sound of that.

"Good," Gage said. "All right, let's take a look. And *Star Mist*, keep the image only for chairmen at the moment."

"First only show Seeder ships and designate this ship with a slightly brighter point," Angie said.

Damn, Benny found this so exciting he had to force himself to breathe.

Gina squeezed his hand and took a deep breath as well.

A hologram of the area of space along the front line appeared in front of Benny and Gina.

Benny was surprised at how many thousands of small green dots appeared around *Star Mist*'s position in space.

It seemed as if their coverage was very tight, but he knew those ships were hundreds of light years from the closest ship, some far more. And without this scanner, up until now they only had short-range scanners of less than a quarter of a light year to try to find an alien ship.

On the left were the alien occupied galaxies, on the right were the galaxies they were trying to protect from the alien ships.

"*Star Mist*, now add in the alien ships," Angie said.

The entire hologram almost turned completely red.

Angie gasped.

Gina clamped down on Benny's hand.

Benny said simply, "Shit."

It was a massive sea of millions and millions of alien ships. And a lot of the red dots were into the galaxies behind the front line.

Benny felt sick.

"We are so screwed," Gage said.

Benny could only agree with that.

"Let's see what it looks like around *Star Rain*," Angie said, her voice almost hollow.

The horrid image vanished and once again Benny forced himself to take a deep breath.

A second hologram appeared in front of them, showing the Seeder ships and *Star Rain*. Again it seemed like a decent defense line.

"*Star Rain*, please add in the alien ships," Benny said.

Again the entire hologram seemed to turn a bright shade of red. And the galaxies beyond the front lines were filled with red dots as well.

Benny just wanted to hit something, but instead he just sat there.

The same thing repeated around *Star Fall*.

And these images showed only a tiny, tiny part of the battle area. They wouldn't have the full picture for years yet until all the scanner boosters were put into place.

But it was clear from where Benny sat.

They were losing this war.

As far as he knew, they had already lost it.

CHAPTER 4

Gina stood beside their chairmen's chair in the command center, just sort of staring at the big screen and thinking. Benny was off having a quick meeting with some military mother-ship chairmen and he was going to meet her back here at any moment.

On the screen in front of her it showed the area of space they had been trying to defend, mostly covered with red alien ships.

For the three years after the first scans, humanity had geared up even more. It seemed that Ray and Tacita were moving mountains, if not entire galaxies, to join the fight. They were pushing to get every bit of fighting power to these front lines.

Gina was impressed and it seemed that those first scans had scared them more than anyone.

Anyone with a brain knew how scary an infestation like this

was. Like a bad infection in a human body could spread, this infection, if not contained at this level, could spread over all the known universe. And at full force, even a galaxy of humans could not stop the wave of rats pouring at them.

After three years, new military ship factories were coming online almost every week around this sector of space.

And all effort was put to building booster scanners and linking in all fighting ships to the scans so they would know if there was an alien ship close to them.

The kill rate of alien ships had jumped dramatically with the ability to see them. The small military ten-man fighters were now being called Sharks because they could take out an alien ship and jump and ten minutes later take out another.

But Gina and everyone on every ship knew they were still losing.

One alien planet alone in a galaxy could pour out millions and millions of transport ships over a fifty-year period, continuing until every bit of material on the planet was exhausted.

You multiply that by maybe a billion planets in just a normal-sized galaxy and hundreds of years and the number became a staggering wave of red.

Gina still felt mostly discouraged at the progress. But after three years they finally had all the area inside the million galaxies in this area monitored in one way or another.

So they at least knew how bad they were losing.

Benny's secondary line of defense which was to protect the galaxies beyond the main line of defense seemed to be on full push as well. But it took far more firepower to destroy a growing infestation on a planet then it did a transport ship in space. So the decision had been made to follow Seeder guidelines and just let the civilization grow once it was started on a planet. But a number of Sharks would be stationed in orbit to make sure no alien ship left the planet's gravity well.

But in every galaxy there could be a billion alien planets. Once infected to any extent, that line of defense flat didn't work.

But on new infections into a galaxy, that plan of Sharks in orbit tended to stop the growth inside of new galaxies when caught early. But they often didn't see a new planet starting to launch ships until the ships were in space and able to be picked up on the scanners.

And often the ship wasn't in space very long jumping between planets, so even with the scanning technology, they didn't have the firepower or even awareness to track everything.

Gina knew, as all of them did, that they were still decades, if not a hundred years or more from having enough ships to even begin to battle this growing infestation on a level basis.

They were slowing the spread, but only slowing it.

And not by that much.

Very discouraging.

The third line of defense was also catching ships now that they could see them.

At one point a few months back, they had decided to set up yet a fourth line of defense much farther out, just to be sure. The sensors for that were being built now.

And Ray and Tacita reported that the sensor shield and thousands of ships were now manning the protection line between this area of space and human occupied space. Even though it would take an alien ship thousands of years to make that journey with the old trans-tunnel drives they used, no one wanted to take a chance that just one ship would get through.

Angie felt good about that at least.

Over the last year, two more Seeder mother ships had arrived as well. But the chairmen of both had no battle experience, so even though considerably older, they chose to let the six chairmen of the three main ships be in charge of the entire operation.

So the weight of all this rested on the six of them. And Gina felt it every day. And she knew Benny did as well.

This was going to be a very, very long fight.

SECTION TWO

THE EMPTY SPACE PROBLEM

CHAPTER 5

Benny and Gina were in their command chair, studying the battle scenes as more sensors came online. Behind them, the huge command center ran with muffled talking and an efficiency Benny always found impressive. They had the best and most dedicated command crew anyone could ever hope for.

And all of them were focused completely on the task at hand, even though they all knew they would be at this for maybe a century or more.

Star Rain fed Benny and Gina information both through non-verbal connections and heads-up displays. The situation had just gotten worse and worse as each day went by, especially now that they actually knew where more and more of the alien ships were.

And it seemed like every day more sensors came onto the network showing millions more alien ships.

Benny hated the impossible feeling of what they were facing. As Carey had said a number of years back, they couldn't miss a single alien ship. But from the sensors they now had online, the rough count of alien ships was far over eighty billion.

He couldn't even imagine that number.

And every day that count seemed to climb instead of go down, even with thousands and thousands of Seeder ships destroying alien ships. It seemed more alien ships were launched from hundreds of millions of planets than Seeder ships could destroy by factors.

The initial mission of the three mother ships to this distant area of space had been to find out about an alien culture. A solo alien ship had reached the edge of human occupied space with its alien occupants long dead. The ship had been traveling for over two hundred thousand years. So no one knew what to expect at the origin of that alien ship.

With the new trans-tunnel drive and exploring along the way, it had taken thirteen years for the three mother ships, *Star Rain, Star Mist,* and *Star Fall* to reach the alien area of space.

When they had first gotten to this area of space, they had discovered hundreds and hundreds of completely destroyed galaxies. It seemed the branch of humanity that had created this mess was trying to destroy the aliens by firebombing every alien planet in an entire galaxy.

But usually by the time The Creators, as they called themselves, had gotten to a galaxy to destroy it, the aliens had already sent out hundreds of millions of ships from that galaxy to infect millions more galaxies.

So when the three mother ships had arrived and learned what was happening, the decision had been made to not even contact The Creators. Or the group that had followed them millions of years before called "The Exterminators." Since both ancient groups still had old, slow drives, it was decided they would be more trouble than they would be help.

The decision of the Seeders was to let the aliens left behind on planets just die off naturally. It seemed the aliens took every resource a planet had to build ships and those left behind on the planet were without food and resources and turned on each other and quickly died off.

So the Seeders had taken the fight to the vastness of space between the galaxies to stop the aliens in space. That had been Benny's idea. But now he was starting to think that idea had no hope.

"*Rescue One* has arrived in the area of *Star Mist*," *Star Rain* reported to them.

Benny glanced at the specs on the newly arrived ship as they scrolled over his display.

Rescue One was half the size of a mother ship and the chairman was named Evan West. *Rescue One* had been upgraded to the new trans-tunnel drive and in the ten-year trip here from human space, it had built complete hangars full of the large military ships and a couple thousand smaller Sharks.

And they had brought the crew for all of the ships as well as the crew for another two hundred ships yet to be built here.

"Wow," Gina said. "That's going to help some."

Benny wanted to say that it wouldn't make a dent, but he didn't. Gina and the other four chairmen who were running this knew exactly how bad the situation was. They were kids on a beach with sand pails trying to stop a tsunami. He didn't need to make things worse by running off his mouth.

Then a bit of data about the new arrival went over his screen. It seemed the *Rescue One* got its name when it was built to save the mother ship *Dreaming Large* from empty space.

He didn't remember learning anything about that.

Now all Seeder ships just had automatic sensors and avoided the small, solar-system-sized bubbles of null or empty space. He did a quick scan of the story about *Dreaming Large*.

It was thanks to that rescue operation the sensors for null space had been invented for every Seeder ship. Before then, Seeder ships just vanished, often not appearing again for hundreds of thousands of years, even though on the ship only a few hours had passed.

Suddenly Benny realized something else they were missing.

Something major.

Empty space.

Damn, just damn.

He brought back up the image of the fifty or so galaxies closest to their position on his and Gina's display. As always, there were a few thousand Seeder ships showing green in a sea of alien red ships. Even though the area shown was more than a hundred million light years across, it still looked like it was covered in solid red.

Gina glanced at him. He could sense she was puzzled at what he was doing.

"*Rescue One* reminded me we are missing something very,

very critical in this fight," he said. "*Star Rain*, please show in bright white dots all the empty space areas in this scan."

The white dots spread out solidly through the entire area of space.

"Oh, no," Gina said, clearly catching on to what he was thinking.

"*Star Rain*," Benny said, "Approximately, to the nearest thousand, how many empty space areas are showing?"

"Over eighty-six thousand," *Star Rain* said.

"*Star Rain*," Gina said, "Would you have any way to estimate how many alien ships have been lost in an empty space bubble?"

"In this area shown?" *Star Rain* asked.

"Yes," Benny said. "In the area shown."

"Approximately nine thousand," *Star Rain* said.

"Could you extrapolate that over the entire history of the alien race expansion," Gina asked. "Very rough and approximate would be fine."

"Aliens have been expanding for 280 thousand years," *Star Rain* said. "In that amount of time, an estimation of alien ships vanishing into null space would be approximately two hundred million."

"Two hundred million?" Gina asked.

"Approximately," *Star Rain* said.

"We are so screwed," Benny said, his stomach in a knot as he stared at the screen of red with white dots. And he had thought the battle had been impossible ten minutes ago.

"We can't miss a ship," Gina said softly.

"Even one that might just reappear two hundred thousand years from now," Benny said.

Gina laughed, but it sounded forced. "At least they are out of our way for now."

Benny laughed. But she did have a point.

CHAPTER 6

Gina hated more than she wanted to think about the empty space problem Benny had just noticed. She had been managing to hold out hope that given enough time and forces, they could slow and then eventually stop the alien expansion.

She knew that was only a hope, and not based on any kind of probability. After the first group of sensors came online, Benny had asked *Star Rain* to calculate the odds of defeating the alien expansion.

Star Rain's answer had been zero percent. Not even a tiny fraction chance of success. Benny had decided he would never ask that question again, but he still did every six months or so.

He just put his head down and worked on the problem, something she loved about him. One of the many hundreds of things she loved about him, actually. No task seemed impossible to him if he worked at it hard enough.

Now this had just made things worse.

Much worse.

One alien ship finding a galaxy and this infection would start all over. Just one.

"We need to tell the others," Benny said after the two of them had gone back over the data even more about how many alien ships were trapped in empty space, just waiting like time-bombs to come out and infect things all over again.

"Not going to be a fun meeting," she said.

"How about we get Chairman West in on the meeting to help us understand everything," Benny said, standing.

Gina stood as well and stretched. "But let's talk with the other four first, so they are not caught by surprise with this."

Benny nodded, then said, "*Star Rain,* would you contact the Chairmen of *Star Fall* and *Star Mist* and ask for an emergency meeting on *Star Mist?*"

"Be glad to," *Star Rain* said.

A moment later *Star Rain* said, "They have agreed. On *Star Mist.*"

"Thank you," Gina said.

A moment later she and Benny were standing in the *Star Mist* conference room more millions of light-years away from *Star Fall* than she wanted to think about.

The large oak-colored wooden table filled the center of the conference room and Gina and Benny took their normal seats along one side in the comfortable dark-leather chairs. She could smell some cookies and cupcakes already on the table at the back, but at the moment she didn't feel up for a snack. Not with this news they were about to hand to the others.

Carey and Matt appeared a moment later and sat across from Gina and Benny. Both Carey and Matt were dressed comfortably in jeans and light shirts.

Gina loved the lack of any dress code about the Seeders. There was never a thought about dressing other than for comfort. She and Benny were seldom in anything but jeans, dress shirts, and tennis shoes. Sure made dressing every morning easier.

"Even more problems, huh?" Matt asked, smiling as he sat down.

"They never seem to end," Benny said, smiling as well.

"Oh, super," Carey said, laughing. "And just when some major reinforcements arrived."

"Yeah," Benny said, "that illustrated the problem."

Gina loved the attitude of the six of them. They all knew it was impossible, what they were trying to do, but they didn't let that get to their attitudes.

At that moment Angie and Gage appeared and sat at the head of the large table.

"More fun, huh?" Gage asked.

"A real party," Benny said.

"So we noticed that the *Rescue One* had arrived," Gina said, deciding to get right to the point.

"Bringing a bunch of military ships and Sharks," Gage said, nodding. "We all just need to figure out how to deploy all of them."

Everyone nodded, but waited for Gina to go on.

"*Rescue One* is known for saving the mother ship *Dreaming Large* from an empty space bubble," Gina said.

"And giving all Seeder ships a scanning system to spot empty space bubbles and avoid them," Benny said.

"Oh, shit," Gage said, sitting back.

Gina nodded. Clearly Gage had jumped to exactly what they had figured out.

"May I have *Star Mist* put up a hologram of this area of space?" Gina asked.

Angie nodded, looking puzzled at Gage who just sat there staring at the ceiling.

"*Star Mist*, would you please show a hologram of the closest 50 galaxies along this line of defense?"

"I would be glad to," *Star Mist* said and the hologram appeared. It looked so clean with just the dots of lights.

"Please show all alien ships in this area of space," Gina said. She didn't really want to see this again for this area, but they all had to.

The clean image became filled with more millions of red dots than Gina wanted to think about it.

"Please, *Star Mist*," Gina said, "would you show the locations in bright white dots of the empty space pockets in this area?"

The white lights appeared, dotted all over the area and all through the red dots of alien ships.

"Oh, no," Angie said.

Carey and Matt were just sitting back, staring at the hologram, their mouths open and their eyes wide.

"*Star Mist*," Gina said, "could you estimate, roughly, the number of alien ships in this scanned area likely to now be caught in empty space pockets?"

"Over ten thousand," *Star Mist* said. "Rough estimation and rounded."

"Thank you, *Star Mist*," Gina said.

Everyone was silent just staring at the hologram full of red and the bright white lights showing pockets of empty space.

"*Star Rain* estimates," Gina said, "that we could have over two hundred million alien ships trapped in empty space pockets since the beginning of the alien expansion."

"Do you agree with that number, *Star Mist?*" Angie asked.

"Yes," *Star Mist* said. "Many factors are in the equation, but taking into account the time of alien expansion and location of many of the empty space bubbles, that number might be slightly low."

Silence filled the conference room as all six of them sat staring at the sector of space filled with red dots of alien ships.

Finally Angie said, "Thank you, *Star Mist*. You can shut down the image."

The image of hopelessness hanging over the table vanished and Gina found herself taking a deep breath.

"I'm so glad you wanted to share this news," Gage said, shaking his head.

"That's what friends are for," Benny said, smiling.

They all laughed. Not one thing else they could do.

CHAPTER 7

Benny liked Chairman Evan West of *Rescue One* right from the start. West was a tall, thin man with bright green eyes and a balding head. From his record, he was thousands of years old, which had Benny intimidated almost from the start.

But when Chairman West transported to the meeting room to talk with the six of them, he was charming and kept the mood light to start. He took a chair at the end of the table facing Angie and Gage.

And West was very, very respectful to all of them, even though combined they hadn't lived a third of his age. That didn't seem to bother him in the slightest.

When he first arrived, it was clear to Benny that Chairman West thought he was here to talk about how to deploy his ships and forces. And they would have that meeting in time.

So when Angie asked him to explain to them the nature of empty space, he looked surprised.

"Your arrival has made us realize we have a problem," Gage said.

"A larger problem than the impossible one we already face," Benny said.

"Yeah, that too," Gage said.

West chuckled, but Benny could tell he was suddenly worried.

"We think," Gage said, "that we have over two hundred million alien ships in empty space bubbles."

West started to say something, then stopped, his mouth open.

Benny could see that suddenly the obvious that they had all missed hit West solidly. No one, since his rescue of *Dreaming Large*, thought much at all about empty space. Like a moon or an asteroid belt, it was just something to not hit.

"We can't let one ship escape," Angie said.

"One ship can contaminate an entire galaxy in just over six hundred years," Carey said, "and launch more hundreds and hundreds of millions of alien ships into space than we want to think about."

"So we need a lesson on empty space bubbles to know what we are facing," Benny said.

Benny watched as Chairman West just blinked for a moment.

"How they are formed, do they serve a purpose, how can we destroy one, and so on," Angie said.

West nodded and took a deep breath.

Benny was impressed. This guy had lived a very long time, but it was clear to Benny he had never been under this kind of stress before, except maybe in the rescue of *Dreaming Large*.

"I can download to your ships from *Rescue One* all data we gathered and details," West said, "to the tiniest detail on how we freed *Dreaming Large*."

"Would you do that now," Angie asked. "We need to have our ships with all this information as soon as possible."

West nodded and contacted his second in command and had that done.

A few moments later *Star Mist* said, "Receiving the information now."

Benny contacted *Star Rain* and Carey contacted *Star Fall* to make sure the information was coming in there as well.

"So," Gina said after a moment, facing Chairman West, "what exactly is empty space?"

"It is, basically," West said, taking a deep breath and focusing on the topic at hand, "exactly what its name implies. It is an area devoid of all space and time. Normal space around us has many things in it, but inside the gravitational bubble of empty space, nothing exists, including most laws of physics."

Benny tried to image that and failed, so decided to ask the next question.

"How does a bubble like that even exist? What creates it?"

"Universal forces of gravity create them," West said. "Every object in the universe warps time and space around it. When certain sets of gravitational forces come into play with each other, the forces form neutral areas and these neutral areas form as gravitational bubbles of nothingness."

Benny shook his head, still not following completely.

"So back on our home world," Matt said, "we had high-speed roads for traffic. These roads formed all sorts of patterns to allow vehicles to get on and off smoothly. But there were always dead, worthless areas inside those interchanges, those patterns."

West nodded. "My home world had those as well. Those dead areas would be these empty space areas. Gravitational forces are in play around a dead area like traffic on an exchange and form the bubble around the nothingness. Once formed it takes on a stability all its own."

Benny shook his head and smiled at Matt. "Thank you. Just saved me a giant headache trying to understand these things."

"I was going there myself," Matt said, smiling.

"Think of them like a balloon," West said. "To save the *Dreaming Large*, we had to let in regular space and time evenly from all directions at the same time."

"So if we just blow a hole in the side of one of these empty spaces?" Benny asked.

"Real time and space and gravitational forces would rush in and destroy anything inside the bubble," West said.

"So we need to pop a lot of bubbles," Benny said, nodding. Maybe, just maybe not all was lost yet.

"We can do that," Gage said and the other chairmen nodded.

"For every bubble you pop," West said, shaking his head, "another might appear to balance things. It seems the bubbles are also used to balance gravitational forces in an area. Or at least that's the theory. Never been tested. Until now there was no reason to test it."

"When you destroyed the bubble around *Dreaming Large*, did another one form?" Angie asked.

West nodded. "About thirty light-years away and almost swallowed another Seeder ship before we realized what was happening and got the ship out of the way."

Benny just shook his head. Nothing at all was easy about any of this.

CHAPTER 8

Gina and Benny had alternated cooking from the moment they had met. They both liked to cook and it gave them time away. They both tried to protect their private time and get full nights sleep every night. And dinner was part of that.

This evening it was Gina's turn and she was working on a pasta salad and chicken breasts smothered in Italian spices. One of the advantages they had being on a ship the size of a moon, there was lots of room to grow fresh vegetables and chicken and fish.

The kitchen in their chairmen's quarters was a dream kitchen as far as she was concerned, with stone-like counter tops, two large sinks, and enough area to prepare anything she or Benny felt like preparing.

Off to one side of the kitchen was a wonderful dining room that could sit eight at the beautiful wooden maple dining table, but they kept the table downsized so she and Benny could sit facing each other and talk across a small table.

They had decorated their apartment with pictures of her home planet and New York City on his home world, where they had lived together for the first two years and tried to help survivors of what they called The Event.

It had been a hard two years, scrambling for food and trying to keep the spirits of those around them up. Even though at any point they could have gone to one of the Seeder ships in orbit, they chose to stay on the surface.

So now those images of her home world and his decorated their wonderful apartment. And in the nearby living room they often cuddled on the couch and watched old movies. She had a lot of movies from his world to catch up on and he had a lot of movies from hers. It was great fun.

She was almost finished with preparing dinner and was about to call Benny when he came out of his office and leaned against the counter to watch her.

"Anything I can do to help?" he asked. "It smells wonderful."

"Just sit down," she said, laughing.

They went through that exact same routine every night, the one not cooking asking at the last minute if they could help. She loved that ritual.

"So what were you working on?" she asked as she first dished up the pasta salad.

"Trying to see if I can understand these empty space bubbles a little more," he said.

"And do you?" she asked, as she put the chicken on a plate

for each of them and decorated it with steamed spears of asparagus.

"I think I do," he said as she served them both and sat down. "But can't seem to find an answer to one really stupid question."

He shook his head and dug into the salad.

"What question," she asked.

"Can we move the things," he said.

She sort of froze, the first bite of chicken halfway to her mouth.

"Move them?"

"Great chicken," he said, nodding.

"Thank you," she said, finishing getting the bite to her mouth. And he was right, it had come out wonderfully, with an Italian spice that gave it just a little zest but kept the chicken flavor.

"So why move them?" she asked.

"Something you said earlier," Benny said. "If we could get more alien ships to run into the empty space on their own, we could slow them down and then we come along later and pop the bubble and destroy bunches of them all at the same time."

She just stared at the man she loved more than anything. He looked more military than anything, yet his mind worked in ways that constantly astounded her.

He could see things that made no sense to anyone else.

"Also trying to see if we could make them bigger," he said. "Bigger rat traps."

She just kept staring at him. Both of those ideas just might work. Both were brilliant and might turn the tide if they did work.

He shrugged and kept eating. "Silly damn idea considering the size of space between galaxies."

She just kept staring at him until he noticed and stopped eating and said, "What? I got food stuck to my nose or something?"

She laughed. "No, just admiring that brain of yours is all."

He laughed. "I'll let you admire other parts of this body later if you want."

"Once I get past admiring the brain," she said, smiling at him, "I just might."

CHAPTER 9

Benny and Gina the next morning in their command chair, after going over all the reports coming in from scouts and Sharks destroying alien ships, decided to dig more into the idea of moving one of the empty space bubbles.

They had talked about it more last night and both spent time in their offices after dinner making sure they understood what these empty space bubbles actually were.

As far as Benny could tell, they were exactly as Chairman West described them. Nothingness. Complete. No time, no gravity, nothing, held together by a gravity bubble membrane of some sort.

And the more they researched it, the more excited Benny got that this might not be another problem, but in fact might be another weapon for them in the fight to stop the alien expansion.

So now after a good night's sleep, they sat in their command chair ready to try to figure it all out.

"*Star Rain?*" Benny asked, "would it be possible to move an empty space bubble?"

"In theory, yes," *Star Rain* said.

Since they were in their command chair, he was holding Gina's hand and he squeezed it in excitement of that answer.

She squeezed back.

"Would it be possible to expand the size of an existing empty space bubble?" Gina asked.

"In theory, yes," *Star Rain* said.

Benny almost felt like jumping up out of the chair and doing a little dance. But he had one more question.

"*Star Rain*, would it be possible to create from scratch an empty space bubble?"

"In theory, yes," *Star Rain* said.

Benny had to get up and so did Gina. They both stood and paced in front of their chair, making many of the command crew look down at them with puzzled looks. But since both were smiling, the command crew, rightfully, decided to not say anything. At that moment, Benny appreciated that.

"Before we go one more step down the road on this," Gina said, finally stopping in front of Benny, smiling, "we need to see if the size of space the alien ships are traveling through would even make such a thing worthwhile to us."

"Agreed," Benny said. "*Star Rain*, on the big screen, please illustrate an alien occupied galaxy with most of the alien inhabited planets in the galaxy producing alien ships. Any of the galaxies that fit that parameter would be fine."

In front of them on the wall-sized screen a three dimensional image of a spiral galaxy appeared. It looked a lot like the Milky Way, only about two-thirds the size from the statistics being shown on the screen.

"How many alien planets in this galaxy?" Gina asked.

The Creators had designed this rat-like race to need a similar planet than humans needed under a yellow star in what was the habitable temperature zone orbit. So that limited the number of planets a great deal.

"Approximately six-point-one billion," *Star Rain* said.

"How many alien ships are leaving this galaxy in a twenty-four-hour period?" Gina asked.

"One-point-four million," *Star Rain* said.

Benny just shook his head. Maybe it would be better to just go in and destroy every planet in the galaxy as The Creators and The Exterminators were trying to do. But he couldn't stomach that and he knew most Seeders could not either, unless it was a last resort.

But at these numbers, unless they found some way to slow down those ships and the alien expansion, Seeders may not have a choice.

"Would you please show, if possible, the general path of most of the ships?" Gina asked.

"Alien ships are designed, from what we have learned from the Creator's files," *Star Rain* said, "to first find the closest planet to settle and then the closest galaxy. In a simple view, these are the three main paths the majority of alien ships are taking from this galaxy."

The image on the screen shifted to looking down on the

galaxy as if it were just in two dimensions. The red dots of alien ships formed three wide streams, going in three directions from the galaxy toward three other galaxies.

Benny just damn near fell over.

"Holy shit," a voice echoed through the room from the command crew behind them.

Benny couldn't agree more.

"So we can predict them to a degree," Gina said, nodding to Benny and smiling.

He just stood there staring at the screen. Then he asked the question he didn't want to ask.

"How wide and how deep are each of those streams of alien ships, approximately?"

Benny was holding his breath waiting for the answer and he bet everyone in the command center behind him was doing the same.

"Each stream is approximately the same width as the galaxy, or 100,000 light years wide," *Star Rain* said, "and the same depth as the galaxy of about 8,000 light years."

"How long is the travel time for an alien ship?" Gina asked. "Please indicate in approximate years near each stream on the screen."

On the screen Benny could see the answer. One stream took approximately 27 years for each ship to get to the next galaxy. Another stream took 30 years, and a third stream took 34 years.

"*Star Rain*," Benny said, "In theory, could we make an empty space bubble a full light year across?"

"In theory, yes," *Star Rain* said.

"How big could we go?" Gina asked.

"There is a stabilization point," *Star Rain* said. "Any size would be possible, in theory, if that stabilization point in the area of the empty space bubble was maintained."

"Holy shit," Benny said to himself.

Gina just grabbed him and kissed him.

Then she turned and said to everyone in the command center, "Go back to work. We'll brief you all on this as soon as we know more."

"*Star Rain*," Benny said, "Could you ask the other four chairmen for an emergency meeting again. And ask them to invite Chairman West."

A moment later *Star Rain* said, "They have agreed."

"Here we go," Gina said.

"I just hope we don't waste too many resources on this," Benny said, suddenly feeling worried. This idea was totally crazy and right now they couldn't afford to go wasting resources in a wrong direction.

"Can we stop a million-plus ships a day just from this one galaxy?" Gina asked.

Benny shook his head. They couldn't even stop a fraction of them, even knowing where they were. And that was only one small galaxy.

"So no idea is too wild to explore," she said, smiling at him. "Even one of yours."

"Thanks," he said, laughing and shaking his head. "I think."

He just hoped to hell she was right.

SECTION THREE

THE SHAPE OF EMPTY SPACE

CHAPTER 10

Gina and Benny had presented what they had discovered and thought about to the other chairmen in the meeting room on *Star Mist*.

At first, the other chairmen had just sat there, stunned. Chairman West just sort of nodded the more they got into their presentation.

Gina and Benny could hardly contain their excitement and Gina could tell the excitement seemed to slowly be catching with the others. These empty-space pockets might not be a huge problem, but instead a weapon.

Then Gage asked simply, once Benny and Gina were finished, "Is this possible?"

"*Star Rain* says it is in theory," Gina said.

All six looked at West.

He shrugged. "Empty space pockets tend to be a certain size, but not all of them. I have seen empty space pockets smaller than a moon and others twenty times the size of the one that caught *Dreaming Large*."

"*Star Mist*," Angie said, "Would you consult with *Star Rain* and *Star Fall* to determine the parameters possible for an empty space bubble?"

"We agree that any size is theoretically possible," *Star Mist* said. "But past a certain size the bubble would only exist for a fraction of a second."

"What is that theoretical size of stability?" Gage asked.

"A diameter of just over one hundred light years," *Star Mist* said.

Gina felt shocked. Putting an empty space bubble that size in the middle of those three major streams would catch millions and millions of alien ships each and actually give the Sharks a chance at slowing down and destroying the remaining ships.

"*Star Mist*, could we create one that size?" Matt asked.

"In theory," *Star Mist* said.

"Do you three ships have any idea or theories on how that could be accomplished?" Angie asked.

"No," *Star Mist* said.

Gina did not like the sound of the finality of that statement. But it didn't seem to bother West in the slightest.

"Let me get my original *Dreaming Large* rescue team on this," he said. "They are the best experts there are on empty space. I'll pull them all back together from all over the human universe. We'll find the answer."

"And moving the smaller ones would help as well," Benny said.

West nodded.

Gina understood what Benny was thinking. He had thought about just sending numbers of the small empty space pockets moving back along a stream from a galaxy, catching ships as it went. He had called it "bowling for aliens" and she had kissed him for that silliness.

But underneath the silliness, it was a good idea.

"Once I distribute the fighting forces I brought with me," West said, jumping into action, "with your permissions, I would like to set up my ship to be the ground center on this research."

Gina glanced around and all were nodding.

"Please do so," Angie said after checking with all the chairmen.

"I will get in touch with Chairmen Ray and Tacita and get their help as well," West said.

Gina could hear the growing excitement in his voice.

Clearly Benny could as well. "You think this is possible?" Benny asked.

West shrugged. "If *Star Mist* and your other ships say it is theoretically possible, then all we have to do is find out how to change that theoretical to reality. It took us a lot of years to go from knowing nothing about empty space to saving a mother ship from it. I think we can do this as well, but it may take years."

"We are going to be at this for years," Gage said, nodding.

Gina agreed with that.

"The more ideas we have to help," Angie said, "the better off we will be in this fight. So thank you, Chairman West, for running with this. Please give us regular updates on your progress."

"Thank you for trusting me with something this important," he said.

They all stood and for the first time in a lot of years, Gina felt lifted by one of the meetings. Everything was still in theory, but theoretical help was more than they had yesterday.

A lot more.

CHAPTER 11

Benny stood beside their command chair, watching the daily reports of the battle scroll across the big screen. Gina was still in the gym working out as she did three mornings a week, letting him be the first in the Command Center. She liked the extra workout time, said it kept her mind sharp.

Around him the others worked, mostly silently, sometimes conferring with each other in normal voices that seemed almost like whispers down near the command chair the room was so big.

It had been over two years since the meeting about the theory of building large empty space bubbles to trap large numbers of alien ships and Benny had given up counting how many years they had been here blowing alien ships out of space.

Chairman West reported his teams' findings every week on advances in empty space work, but it seemed to Benny to always be the same.

Nothing yet.

Chairmen Ray and Tacita had entire fleets of ships headed this direction, and factories around this area were producing Shark-sized fighting ships at the pace of fifty per day.

The war effort in the last two years had exploded into full movement.

Around Benny, the main command crew was all at stations and working. The entire sphere around the main one hundred and fifty thousand alien-infested galaxies was now under scan, so at least they knew where every alien ship was.

And every alien ship that managed to get outside of that sphere had been destroyed.

But there were far, far too many alien ships to even pretend to deal with, but at least humanity knew where they all were, for what little good that did. Humanity was still losing the battle against the alien expansion and there was talk that in a couple of years they would be forced to fall back to a larger sphere of defense.

That was going to feel like defeat to Benny, but it more than likely was going to have to be done.

Benny was about to turn to talk with their second in command when *Star Rain* said simply, "There is a problem with The Creators' fleet."

Benny glanced back at the big screen. The Creators' ships were working in their area of defense and were always shown as a tiny blob of blue dots moving slowly from galaxy to galaxy. When they reached an alien galaxy, The Creators would fire-bomb every alien planet in the galaxy over a six-week period and then move on, leaving the galaxy a dead husk.

That cleared out and stopped the aliens, but by the time The Creators did that, millions and millions of alien ships had already launched to other galaxies.

Benny considered what The Creators were doing horrid and a total waste of effort. But that was no surprise because The Creators were the same idiots who had started this entire mess with their ideas that they could build an intelligent alien race.

No Seeder had even talked to The Creators. Benny and Gina mostly just ignored them and Benny doubted the Creators even knew the Seeders were here fighting their fight.

The Creators still had the old trans-tunnel drive, so their ships were no faster than the ones they had programmed the aliens to build.

It took Benny a moment of staring at the big screen filling one wall of the command center before he finally understood the problem with The Creators' small fleet of seven-hundred-plus ships.

It was gone.

No blue lights left on the board.

Not a one.

Just Seeder green lights and hundreds of millions of alien red lights.

"*Star Rain*, what happened to The Creators' ships?" Benny asked.

"The entire fleet of Creators' ships," *Star Rain* said, "ran into an empty space pocket about twice the size of the empty space pocket that held the *Dreaming Large*."

Benny just started laughing.

And after a moment most of the command center crew laughed with him.

Irony was a bitch, that was for sure.

CHAPTER 12

Gina found the meeting with the other four mission command chairmen and Ray and Tacita and Chairman West fun and somewhat funny. All of them thought the fact that The Creators' ships had run into an empty space bubble just laughable.

They were all in the *Star Mist* meeting room, as normal. Everyone in the room was dressed casually in jeans, light shirts, and tennis shoes except for Ray and Tacita. Both of them were in their standard black silk.

As far as Gina could tell through the laughter, the consensus of the nine was to leave The Creators' fleet in the bubble. The idiot Creators wouldn't even know any time had passed for a hundred thousand years or so.

After some laughing, a wonderful relief for these meetings, it was Matt who finally pointed out that their method of destroying entire galaxies of aliens was helping a little, even though none of them in the room agreed or liked The Creators' method.

Or liked the fact that they had caused all this in the first place, but Gina didn't say that. She knew they were all thinking it, though.

Ray nodded. "Our simulations show that given enough time, having The Creators and The Exterminators doing what they are doing might be the difference in the final outcome."

"A very slight difference," Tacita said.

Gina could tell that Tacita was just disgusted at The Creators and had no intention of hiding it.

Gina hated to admit that she agreed with that feeling.

"So are you suggesting we let those idiots out of there?" Benny asked.

Gina could tell from Benny's voice that he was surprised at the idea.

"Actually," West said, "It might be a great experiment for us to free them and get more data at the same time. It has been a very long time since we freed the *Dreaming Large*."

Gina nodded to that. Anything at all that would speed up the development of control over empty-space bubbles would be a good thing. Even letting the idiots who caused this entire fight free again.

Ray nodded as well, but Tacita just looked more disgusted.

"Could we free them and not have them spot us?" Matt asked.

Ray and West both shook their heads.

"I'm afraid that wouldn't be possible," West said. "We

would need to surround the bubble and their fleet and they would see us instantly when the bubble dropped."

"So we leave them," Angie said, "or rescue them and tell them we are here trying to clean up their mess."

"Pretty much those two options," Ray said.

"If they have to see us," Gage said, "at least can we direct them toward some alien galaxies that their destruction tactics would make more sense against?"

"That would help," Ray said, nodding.

Gina wasn't sure, but she thought she heard Tacita snort softly.

"So," Carey said, "it seems pretty clear that none of us really want to free those idiots. Correct?"

Gina looked around and everyone was nodding, including Ray. Tacita's head was almost bobbing, she was nodding so hard.

"But," Carey said, "it would give us a bubble release to study for West and his team if we freed them."

West nodded. "A very good example, actually."

"And," Carey said, "in the long run of the war, if we directed them, they might be able to help in a slight way with the overall outcome. Do I have all that correct?"

Everyone nodded again.

Since it was the six of them running this entire operation, even though Ray and Tacita and West and numbers of other chairmen with ships now in the fight had seniority, only the six of them voted on any major decision.

And lately it had been Gina who had polled the six of them. She never polled unless she was sure of the outcome and right now she was sure. They had no other choice that she could see if they hoped to win this war.

"Angie?" Gina said.

"We release them."

"Gage?"

He nodded and shrugged. "Makes sense to release them."

"Carrie?" Gina asked.

Gina could tell that Carey wanted no part of this vote, but she finally glanced at Matt and then said, "Release them."

"I agree," Matt said.

Gina looked at Benny and smiled. "Well?"

"Can we put them back into a bubble when this is all over?" Benny asked.

Gina and everyone laughed, and West said, "We get control of the empty space bubbles, I think that could be arranged without them even realizing they were in one."

"Then we release them for now," Benny said.

"I agree," Gina said, laughing. "For now."

"I think after the mess they have caused," Tacita said, "an empty space bubble is where they eventually belong."

Ray nodded to that and everyone else laughed.

CHAPTER 13

"Have I said how much I hate this?" Benny asked as he stood next to Gina in their command center.

On the big screen was showing fifty small Seeder ships and *Rescue One*, Chairman West's ship. They were stationed at regular intervals in a globe form and Benny knew that in that globe shape was an empty space bubble holding an entire fleet of ships. The bubble was about ten times larger than a normal-sized solar system.

"Over the last six months?" Gina said, laughing, "I could have *Star Rain* count the times you have said that, because the number is far too big for me."

Benny shook his head and stared at the screen. "I don't care, I still hate this."

They had moved *Star Rain* to a position near the empty-space bubble holding The Creators' fleet. And when the fleet appeared after West and his people shut down the bubble, it was up to Benny and Gina to explain what had happened and what was going on in the battle against the aliens.

At first Benny thought it would be better to have Ray and Tacita talk with these people, since they were the ones that had sent them off into space to keep humanity safe. But both Ray and Tacita said there would be no point in bringing up old fights.

Million-year-old fights.

Benny thought that too stupid for words, but since The Creators were blowing up galaxies worth of planets in Benny and Gina's area of defense, it fell to them to do the meet and greet.

"Here we go," Chairman West said. "All systems show green. Everyone stand ready."

Benny and Gina turned and sat in their command chairs and *Star Rain* took over feeding them information across their screens. The Creators were going to be in for a shock since *Star Rain* was about four times the size of The Creators' biggest mother ship.

And when the ships were free, *Rescue One* and all of the smaller ships would jump to the new trans-tunnel flight and just vanish as far as The Creators' sensors would know.

"Permission to go?" Chairman West asked Benny and Gina.

Benny glanced at Gina and she nodded.

"Go," Benny said.

"*Star Rain*," Benny said, "stand ready to get us out of here instantly at any sign of trouble."

"Understood," *Star Rain* said.

"Mission is a go," Chairman West said.

A moment later an invisible bubble lit up as hundreds of thousands of small explosions spaced evenly around the empty space bubble punctured a hole in the gravitational membrane.

A moment later The Creators' fleet appeared.

West and his smaller ships vanished, leaving only *Star Rain* facing the fleet.

Benny studied the ships.

Seven-hundred-plus small ships, and all of them looked well-used. Four larger ships, three that he knew were nothing more than factory ships to build the explosives to blow up planets and build more small ships. The largest ship was the lead mother ship.

Luckily there were no alien ships also trapped in this bubble. Benny and Gina had a few dozen Sharks standing off ready in case there had been.

The Creators' fleet floated in space.

Benny and Gina just sat there, waiting.

From the perspective of The Creators' fleet, their trans-tunnels drives had suddenly shut down, then a moment later fifty ships surrounded them and then vanished, leaving only one big ship.

Six months had passed since the fleet had gone into the bubble, but to them it had only been a few seconds at most. So Benny and Gina were under no illusion that this was going to be a very interesting meeting.

"We are being hailed by the mother ship *Stahl*," *Star Rain* said.

"On our screens and the main screen," Gina said.

"Language translation complete," *Star Rain* said. "You will be speaking the language on the ship you are talking with."

"Thank you, *Star Rain*," Gina said.

An instant later a woman who looked to be about thirty, as all Seeders looked, appeared. She had dark brown hair chopped short and dark brown eyes. Her nose was long and her eyes set slightly too close together.

Benny and Gina had their image sent to her as well.

"I am Chairman Havemann of the mother ship *Stahl*," she said. "May I inquire as to what just happened and who you might be?"

Benny and Gina had decided that if the captain was a man, he would talk, if a woman, Gina would talk.

"Chairmen Slade and Helm of the Seeder mother ship *Star Rain*," Gina said. "You and your fleet were trapped for the last six months in an empty-space bubble. We just freed you."

"Six months?" Havemann asked.

She glanced around and clearly someone behind her confirmed that six months of time had passed. She turned back and Benny almost laughed at how her face had gone pale.

"I owe you our thanks," she said, bowing slightly.

Benny was surprised. From what Ray and Tacita had said, he did not expect any kind of courtesy or respect from anyone in this fleet.

"You are more than welcome," Gina said.

Benny could tell that Gina was surprised as well at the courtesy.

"You are Seeder?" Havemann said. "We only know of you as ancient myth."

That surprised Benny as well, but Ray and Tacita had warned them that might be the case.

"None of your original Creators remain?" Gina asked, her voice level.

Havemann frowned. "I do not understand why you would call us Creators?"

"Didn't you create this race you are trying to stop?" Gina asked.

"We did that," Havemann said, nodding with a sad look on her face. "Our ancestors over four hundred generations removed let an experiment get out of hand and we have spent every moment since trying to stop the expansion of the experiment."

Benny opened his mouth to say something, but Gina squeezed his hand and he didn't say a word. It was clear to him that these Creators did not live long lifespans like normal Seeders.

In fact, from his quick math of the time since the alien expansion started, these ships were full of just regular life-span humans.

That was something Ray and Tacita had not warned them about. It seemed that the Seeder long-life gene was very rare and was not passed down or activated on these Creators' ships over the millions of years.

So everyone on the ships had been born on the ships and would die on the ships. They had been fighting these aliens for four hundred plus generations.

Benny just felt stunned at that thought.

The Creators were humans, not Seeders.

CHAPTER 14

Gina was doing her best to maintain a calm, collected outer face when talking with Chairman Havemann, but she knew she needed to collect herself a little more and talk with the other chairmen before going on. This meeting was not at all what she had expected.

"Do you have the history of your voyage in space?" Gina asked.

Chairman Havemann shook her head. "We do not. The first part and why we were in space in the first place was lost right after what is known as the 'awakening.' We do not honestly know what that even means."

Gina had a hunch she knew and right now she really, really needed to have a few words with Ray and Tacita.

Maybe forceful words.

Gina smiled at Chairman Havemann. "May I beg your indulgence and ask for a short break. It will give you time to make sure your fleet is fully functional and allow me to consult with others as to what information we can give you."

Chairman Havemann looked puzzled, but nodded. "Of course."

"Thank you," Gina said and cut the connection.

"What the hell is going on?" Benny asked as they both stood.

"That's exactly what we need to find out," Gina said. "*Star Rain*, please ask the other chairmen for an emergency meeting on *Star Mist* and include Chairmen Ray and Tacita."

"They have agreed," *Star Rain* said a moment later.

Gina took Benny's hand and a moment later they were in the *Star Mist* conference room. Gina knew that the other chairmen and Ray and Tacita had listened to the meeting.

Ray and Tacita were sitting at their end of the table when Benny and Gina appeared.

A second later the other four chairmen appeared as well.

"So what didn't you think to tell us about The Creators, as you called them?" Gina asked, not even trying to keep the anger out of her voice.

"What did you do to sabotage their ship?" Benny asked.

Gage was still standing as well. "That's why you were surprised that they were here. You didn't expect them to live much longer after they awoke, did you?"

"We did not," Tacita said, her voice as cold and low as Gina had ever heard it. "And these aliens we are fighting that they created is the reason we tried to do what we did."

"And we succeeded," Ray said. "In what we tried."

"We should have blown their ships out of space," Tacita said.

Gina just shook her head, ignoring the anger coming from Tacita. "You sabotaged their ship to destroy their records after they awoke, right?"

"We did," Ray said, nodding.

"And you made sure their Seeder genes would go dormant while they slept, correct?" Gage asked.

"We did," Ray said, nodding. "We expected them to settle on a planet and just go from there. It felt like a humane thing to do and still stop their mission."

"We never expected them to continue on in space," Tacita said.

"That was why when we realized who they were," Ray said, "we assumed our attempt at sabotaging their Seeder genes had failed and that many of the original crew would be still alive."

"That was why we did not want to talk with them," Tacita said. "Or even contact them. We held nothing back from you."

"We had no idea we had succeeded," Ray said. "Yet failed to stop them at the same time."

"The fact that hundreds and thousands of generations would have stayed on those ships never occurred to us," Tacita said. "Otherwise we would have told you that was possible."

"What about The Exterminators' fleet?" Gage asked.

"We did the same with them," Tacita said.

"We could take no chances that something like this might happen," Ray said.

"In that we failed," Tacita said.

Ray nodded and both of them looked down at the table.

Gina just felt washed out.

She dropped into a chair and Benny sat down hard beside her.

How stupid was this? They now had two fleets of humans flying from galaxy to galaxy destroying millions of alien-rat-infested planets.

What the hell could she even tell the humans?

Beside her Benny looked around at the chairmen in the room. "That fleet of humans, who are doing nothing more than trying to clean up a mess their distant ancestors caused, will need some sort of answers. Anyone have any bright ideas?"

Gina glanced around the room at all the shaking heads.

Great.

Just great.

CHAPTER 15

The eight chairmen talked for over a half hour before finally deciding to do nothing for now.

Benny felt disgusted about that, but at least he won on giving the human ships, both fleets, better information. And telling them that the Seeders were also fighting to stop the aliens.

Everyone agreed that should be done.

He and Gina returned to *Star Rain* and got into their command chair. Then they had *Star Rain* contact Chairman Havemann again.

Benny had promised Gina he would try to keep his mouth shut. He had no doubt that was going to be difficult at best.

"Sorry for the interruption, Chairman" Gina said. "We had to consult with others before moving forward."

Chairman Havemann nodded, clearly puzzled, but said nothing.

"We are from a branch of humans called Seeders," Gina said. "Our ship and many others are here from occupied human galaxies to try to stop these aliens your ancestors created."

"Occupied human galaxies?" Havemann asked, looking puzzled.

"Humans fill many millions of galaxies now," Gina said.

Benny was shocked. For a moment he thought Chairman Havemann might break down right there. But somehow the Chairman held it together. But clearly what Gina had said went against much of what those on the ships had learned over the centuries.

"We believed the two fleets were alone in space," she said. "And we have been unable to find a planet over centuries that we wanted to settle."

"You are far from alone," Gina said. "Right now we have over sixty thousand Seeder ships here fighting the alien expansion, with more coming every month from human galaxies."

"How far is the nearest human galaxy?" Havemann asked, almost breathless.

Benny felt bad. This poor woman and the millions who followed her were doing their best.

"It would take your fleet two-hundred-thousand years to make the journey," Gina said.

"Oh," Havemann said.

Benny felt very bad for Havemann at that point. To a human with a normal life-span, as he thought he had not that many years before, two-hundred-thousand years was difficult to even imagine.

Hell, he couldn't imagine it yet.

"We can discuss all that later," Gina said, moving on. "But right now we need you and your fleet to continue what you are doing. But we can help you pinpoint galaxies in early alien growth instead of later alien growth."

Chairman Havemann nodded.

Benny could see her doing her best to focus back on the task at hand.

"That would help all our morale," Chairman Havemann said.

"My ship is sending you now the next five galaxies you are close to that we need you to take care of," Gina said. "We have decided to fight the alien ships as they leave galaxies."

"Are you in contact with the other fleet?" Chairman Havemann asked.

"We are not," Gina said. "Are you?"

"Yes, we are working together as best we could over such vast distances. They were very worried at our sudden silence for six months."

"My ship is sending you the data of galaxies the other fleet can attack to be more helpful," Gina said. "Please relay the information to them."

Chairman Havemann nodded. "I will."

"Thank you," Gina said. "We will be in regular contact and update you on the status of the battle as it goes on."

"You clearly can see a bigger picture than we can," Havemann said, looking first at Gina, then at Benny.

Benny, with that one look, could see why this woman was the leader of her fleet. She was intense and very smart.

Gina nodded.

"What is the status of stopping the alien expansion?" Havemann asked.

"We are losing," Gina said.

Benny would have tried to say that in a less-blunt fashion.

Havemann nodded.

Benny didn't think she seemed surprised.

"But we have a lot more help on the way," Gina said. "Given time we will wipe your ancestors' experiment from the stars."

"Thank you for that," Havemann said. "Please allow us to help in any fashion we can."

Gina nodded. "For now, continue onward. That's all any of us can do."

"Thank you for the rescue," Havemann said. "And for letting us know you are here with us."

"We will be in touch again soon," Gina said, nodding.

She cut the connection.

Then Gina said to *Star Rain*, "Jump us out of here and back to our home position."

Benny glanced at Gina. He could tell she was very, very upset.

And Benny wasn't feeling that happy either. A group of humans were fighting an impossible fight against all odds to fix a mistake that distant ancestors had made and stupid politics from millions of years before blocked the Seeder's ships from helping them in any real way.

If Benny had anything to say about that, that million-year-old stupid policy was going to change and change soon.

And as upset as Gina felt beside him, that change would happen sooner rather than later.

And maybe then, just maybe, those millions of humans in that fleet and the second fleet might actually get a chance to stop.

But first, there was a war to win.

SECTION FOUR

EVEN MORE HELP

CHAPTER 16

Gina loved how sometimes Benny's thinking would show them ways of doing things they had not thought about before. But more often than not, he just pointed out a missing problem they had to deal with.

The year after they had saved the human fleet from the empty space, Benny and Gina were reading morning reports while in their command chair. Benny had cooked them both a wonderful cheese omelet for breakfast and both had spent an hour exercising.

For the past year, more and more fighting help had poured into the battle from human occupied parts of known space. But Gina and everyone knew they were still losing the overall fight.

And Gina saw no real chance that would change anytime into the near future.

And so far there had been no real progress on the empty-space bubble research, although Chairman West of *Rescue One* reported the research was ramping up wonderfully.

Gina had become friends with Chairman Havemann of the human Creators fleet and had been helping them where she could. The more she got to know Havemann and the humans in that fleet, the more she had come to respect them, even though it was their ancestors who had started this entire mess.

Every month, Gina gave a report to the other chairmen about the human fleet, slowly swaying all of them to a position of willingness to help them.

The human fleet had changed course toward the new galaxy Gina and the Seeders had suggested, and the human fleet was still fourteen years from reaching that target.

"Ever noticed how many alien ships just miss their target?" Benny asked, seemingly out of the blue.

Benny pointed out one alien ship on the report that had been spotted far outside the lines of defense. It had been lost and traveling for almost thirty thousand years. Its occupants were long dead, since the aliens had no way to save themselves when a ship malfunctioned.

Gina had only nodded to that, not really paying much attention, until Benny asked *Star Rain* a question.

"*Star Rain*, would it be possible to estimate how many alien ships miss their target?"

"It would be possible," *Star Rain* said.

Gina looked at her partner and the man she loved more than she could ever love another person. Benny was just nodding. She wasn't sure where he was headed with this sort of questioning.

"*Star Rain*," he said, "with the information we now have about alien ships, how long could the aliens on a ship survive in space without finding a new planet?"

"Extreme outside limit would be one-hundred-thousand years," *Star Rain* said. "The occupants of the ship found near the Milky Way galaxy had survived almost that long."

"Logical amount of time," Benny asked.

"It would be unlikely," *Star Rain* said, "for the alien occupants to survive beyond twenty-thousand years. Most would not make it that long."

Gina still wasn't certain why Benny was asking these questions, but she let him go. She had learned early on in their relationship that when he had his mind on a line of thought, it was better to let him just run down the line to the end.

"Wow," Benny said to himself, shaking his head. "*Star Rain*, would you have an estimation of a failure rate of the alien ships?"

"The construction of the aliens ships is so basic in its nature," *Star Rain* said, "the failure rate is very low. Estimated at less than one-hundredth of a percent."

Gina felt suddenly very thankful for that, since once an alien ship found a planet, it was not used again. The aliens were not able to continue to reuse old ships, they only knew how to build new ones.

"*Star Rain*, since the start of the alien expansion," Benny said, "taking into account the increased numbers of alien ships as time went on the best you can, would you give a general, and I understand rough, estimate of the number of alien ships that have malfunctioned."

"The number," *Star Rain* said, "using every guideline we know to this point about alien ships, would be approximately two-hundred-million alien-ship failures."

Gina just shook her head. Nothing about this battle ever seemed to work out in small numbers. But she still wasn't sure where Benny was going with this line of questions, so she kept quiet.

"*Star Rain*," Benny said, "I am assuming many of those failures would be in the lifting from a planet's gravity well, other failures would be in trying to land on a new planet. Am I correct in assuming such a thing?"

"Yes," *Star Rain* said. "Almost all failures would occur on the alien ship's attempt at landing on a destination planet."

"Over the entire time of alien expansion, would you estimate how many alien-ship failures would cause them to miss the galaxy they were aiming at, as the alien ship did that was found near the Milky Way?"

"Under one-hundred thousand," *Star Rain* said.

Gina felt her stomach twist up into a knot. Now she understood exactly what Benny was trying to find out. The dead alien ship that had been reported today would have been one of those ships.

"How likely would it be for one of those ships," Benny asked *Star Rain*, "with navigation malfunction, to safely land on a planet in another galaxy?"

"Extremely unlikely," *Star Rain* said.

"But still possible?"

"Yes," *Star Rain* said.

"Shit," Gina said softly.

"I'm going to need to see this on the big display," Benny said, squeezing Gina's hand and standing.

Gina stood with him.

Behind them the command center just functioned in its normal soft talk among a few of the crew.

"*Star Rain*," Benny said, "please show an image of the known universe within a twenty-thousand-year standard trans-tunnel drive diameter from the alien expansion start as the center. Please figure in the years since the start of that expansion."

A massive cloud of white dots filled the air above Gina. Each dot was a galaxy.

Behind her all movement and talking of the command crew stopped.

"All it would take would be one ship," Benny said softly.

Gina stared at the massive cloud of a billion galaxies. She needed to ask yet another question.

"*Star Rain*, would it be possible to narrow down likely alien infestation areas from what we know of the alien expansion patterns from each galaxy? If so, please show us those."

Huge amounts of the vast cloud of galaxies vanished, leaving what looked like spokes of a wheel radiating from this area of space.

Twenty spokes, twenty major paths likely taken by malfunctioning alien ships.

"Is it likely that a malfunctioning alien ship found a new planet along one of those paths?" Benny asked.

"No, not likely," *Star Rain* said. "Thirty decimal places below one percent chance."

"But possible?" Gina asked.

"Yes," *Star Rain* said.

Behind Gina she could tell a few of the command crew had picked up on the problem by soft swear words or a slight gasp.

"Ahh, the fun just continues," Benny said, shaking his head.

All Gina could do was stare at the millions of possible galaxies in the star cloud in front of her that might already be infected with aliens.

She didn't consider any of this fun.

CHAPTER 17

Benny knew what they had to do after his little question and answer session with *Star Rain*. They needed, without delay, to send out small fleets of ships along those spoke lines, spread out enough and with the new long-range sensors, to look for alien ships that had missed and were out there.

And those ships along the way needed to pop every empty space bubble they came across to make sure no alien ship was lurking like a bad bomb in one of them.

Given enough time and enough firepower and a lot of luck, Benny believed the aliens could be contained and then destroyed in this area of space.

But if one alien ship got out, found a new planet to infest, and was spreading out there somewhere, that infestation needed to be found and stopped.

He presented his thinking to the other five chairmen on the

same afternoon. All agreed with him. And left it to him and Gina to pick the form of the fleets and the head of each fleet.

Benny figured each fleet could consist of one military mother ship capable of holding five hundred of the ten-man Sharks.

With the Sharks spread out, they could scan a vast amount of space along the likely trails of alien ships. And there would be enough ships to rotate back into the mother ship regularly.

Gina really liked that plan and so did the other chairmen.

The alien ships would take thirty thousand years to travel a certain distance, but with the new trans-tunnel drive, the small military fleet could make the same journey in less than a year.

So Benny and Gina figured they only needed five fleets and could get the job mostly done in less than ten years.

Even Ray and Tacita thought the idea worth the ships and the time.

So only one month after Benny came up with the idea, he and Gina wished Chairman June of the military mother ship *Deep Cycle* good hunting.

The other five fleets left over the next three months.

And except for the weekly reports all the chairmen got, Benny thought nothing much more about those small fleets for the next eleven months. The fleets had found and destroyed a number of stray ships under power, and found no infestations at all along the way.

And they had popped thousands and thousands of the empty-space bubbles without finding a ship either.

But eleven months and six days after *Deep Cycle* left, Benny and Gina got an emergency message from Chairman June.

Chairman Constance June was a bright-eyed woman with long red hair, white skin with freckles, and a biting sense of humor that Benny liked.

Benny and Gina sat in their command chair and told *Star Rain* to keep the communication private for the moment.

Chairman June's face appeared and Benny was shocked. The woman seemed to have not slept in a very long time from the looks of her eyes and her hair had come loose from how she normally tied it back from her face.

"Chairman," Gina said, "what happened?"

"We found an infestation," Chairman June said. "At this point it's held to about fifty galaxies as far as we can tell."

Benny just shook his head. Exactly what he had been afraid of.

Exactly.

"Oh, no," Gina said. Then she said, "Chairman, please send all your data to *Star Rain* now."

Chairman June turned and nodded.

A moment later *Star Rain* said, "I have received the data."

"Is the infestation containable?" Benny asked *Star Rain*.

"It is," *Star Rain* said.

"Containing is not the issue," Chairman June said. "Take a look at this."

Replacing Chairman June's face an image appeared.

The image was of an alien ship powering through deep space between galaxies. Then another ship with a slightly saucer shape and what almost looked like a tail, like a sting-ray in an ocean, came in from the side and with one shot destroyed the alien ship.

If Benny hadn't been firmly held with the form-fitting command chair, he would have gone over backwards.

"What the hell was that?" Benny asked.

"Another group fighting the alien infestation," Chairman June said.

"Humans?" Gina asked.

Chairman June shook her head.

Benny could see the Chairman was almost in shock. "They have a slight humanoid shape, large heads, no nose or ears, large eyes, and are very short and thin."

A moment later a picture of the new alien appeared on the screen.

Chairman June had been correct. Huge head, large round eyes, triangle-shaped head.

Benny didn't find them repulsive as he had some aliens found over the millions of years by Seeder scout ships. Nothing at all like the rat-like aliens they were fighting.

"Not possible," Gina said. "Those are called the Grays on my home planet."

"Mine as well," Chairman June said.

And suddenly Benny realized where he had seen images of these aliens. On television, back on Earth, before the Event destroyed most everything. They had supposedly visited Earth or something like that. He had never paid much attention to that sort of stuff.

Now he wished he had.

Who knew he was going to need it?

CHAPTER 18

Gina forced herself to take a deep breath and think.

What they had discovered wasn't possible by all Seeder records, yet it was happening. The Grays were seemingly fighting an infestation of the aliens.

"Do the Grays know you are there?"

Chairman June shook her head. "We have remained shielded and all Sharks have pulled back inside."

"Good thinking," Benny said. "What kind of capability do the Gray ships have?"

"They have standard trans-tunnel drive is all, but they seemed to be able to pinpoint alien ships, so they must have decent scanners," Captain June said. "They are using the same strategy we are using in letting the aliens have a galaxy once infested, but destroying any alien ship that leaves the galaxy."

Gina was glad to hear that at least.

"Could you tell the size of their fleet?" Benny asked.

"A half-million ships approximately," Chairman June said. "And more seem to be coming from the direction on the other side of this alien infestation."

"Do they seem to be winning against the aliens?" Gina asked.

"Our calculations show that they are not," Chairman June said.

"*Star Rain?*" Benny asked. "From the data sent to you, are the Grays winning against the alien infestation?"

Chairman June is correct," *Star Rain* said. "The Grays stand a zero percent chance against the alien infestation."

"Yet we can defeat it?" Gina asked.

"We can," *Star Rain* said.

Gina glanced at Benny who looked at her and nodded.

"Chairman June," Gina said. "Please hold your position and continue to feed *Star Rain* information as you get it."

Chairman June nodded.

"We will be back to you shortly," Benny said.

Chairman June's face vanished to be replaced with an image of the new alien infestation. Compared to what they were fighting here, it was very small.

"*Star Rain*," Gina said, "please contact *Star Mist* and *Star Fall* and ask for an emergency meeting."

"Also invite Chairman Ray and Tacita," Benny said.

Benny and Gina both stood.

"They have agreed," *Star Rain* said a moment later.

"I need to find something out before this meeting," Benny said to Gina.

Benny turned to the thirty friends that was their command crew. He had come to know and respect and trust all of them.

"Honest show of hands," Benny said, "how many of you on your home worlds heard of aliens called the Grays with big heads and big eyes?"

About three quarters of the command crew raised their hands and then looked at the others around them, surprised.

Benny just shook his head. "There is something very fishy going on. What smells like fish, looks like fish, and tastes like fish, must be fish."

Gina just shook her head. "Want to bet it's just another part of history no one bothered to tell us about."

"No damn bet," Benny said.

CHAPTER 19

Benny was getting damn tired of not being told things and being fed history in bits and pieces like a kid who didn't really need to know things. That just made running a massive war like this dangerous.

If the Grays were spotted on so many human planets in so many different galaxies, it was clear there was much more to their presence here than met the eye.

When Benny and Gina arrived in the conference room, Angie and Gage were already in their chairs, as were Ray and Tacita. Carey and Matt were just pulling out their chairs.

"So we got a fun report from Chairman June of the *Deep Cycle*," Benny said as he and Gina sat down. "Seems they found an alien infestation."

Benny decided he wanted to see what kind of reaction he was going to get from Ray and Tacita.

"Oh, shit," Gage said, sitting forward.

"What we were worried about," Gina said, nodding. "Spread to about fifty galaxies and *Star Rain* tells us we can contain it from the data Chairman June sent us."

"Good," Ray said, nodding.

Benny watched as everyone nodded, clearly surprised at the news, but relieved at the fact that the outbreak could be contained.

"But we have one interesting problem," Gina said.

Benny laughed, pretending he wasn't really annoyed. "Interesting describes it. Seems the outbreak is already being fought by the Grays."

Tacita actually jerked and Ray sat back, clearly shocked. In fact, for as old as those two were, that statement rocked them more than Benny had seen them rocked before.

"Grays?" Gage said.

"Are you talking about the mythical aliens that supposedly visited our Earth?" Angie asked. "The ones with the big heads, big eyes, and little tiny bodies?"

"One and the same," Benny said, nodding.

"We polled our command crew and three quarters of them, from many different galaxies, had heard rumors of the Grays."

"What the hell?" Matt asked, turning to look at Ray and Tacita.

"Now what haven't you told us?" Gage asked.

"I'm sick and tired of being kept in the dark all the time," Angie said, staring at Ray and Tacita.

Benny wasn't surprised at the anger. He was feeling it as well.

Ray and Tacita just sat there, shaking their heads. Both of them were a long way from their eyes.

Finally Ray sort of took a deep breath and looked at Tacita. "A fleet of them must have followed The Creators and The Exterminators."

Tacita nodded. "It would be the only explanation."

"How many ships do they have in the fight?" Ray asked.

"Estimated at about a half million with more coming from the other side of the infestation," Benny said.

That wouldn't be a group just following them," Ray said, clearly puzzled. "This must be closer to their home space."

Benny didn't much like the sound of that at all.

"Ships like saucers with tails?" Tacita asked.

"Yes," Benny said. Then he said simply, "We're all just sitting here waiting for an explanation and why we were never told of these aliens? We were always told there were no other galaxy-spanning race but humans out here."

Ray looked at Tacita and she shrugged.

"We had a treaty with the Grays," Ray said, turning to face the six angry chairmen. "We would wipe their presence from our history, tell no one of their existence, and they would help us in our seeding of galaxies."

Benny glanced at Gina who just sat there clearly still angry.

"Back up to the start," Benny said. "But first, are you telling me that chairmen of mother ships don't even know about the Grays?"

"There are less than one hundred Seeders in all the known universe that know of their existence," Tacita said.

"It has been the best kept secret in all of humanities history," Ray said.

"Seems that secret has sort of hit the bright light of day now," Gage said.

Ray and Tacita said nothing.

"So why the big secret about this treaty?" Angie asked.

"Because it was the Grays that rescued us on the very first Earth from destroying ourselves," Tacita said softly.

Benny sat back so hard, the chair rocked.

"They helped us to survive," Ray said, "but then made us promise we would never help another alien race. It seems they looked on us as a mistake."

Benny wanted to say, You mean like the aliens we are fighting are a mistake. But he didn't.

CHAPTER 20

The silence in the conference room felt like a thick cloud that made it hard to breathe. Gina pushed back from the table some and just forced herself to breathe. Then she broke the silence with a question. "How much older are the Grays than humanity?"

"No one knows," Ray said. "They did not originate in our original galaxy, we do know that. They were only coming through when we were emerging from the original Earth."

"They may look slightly humanoid," Tacita said, "but they are a silica-based life form. They live in dry regions of Earth-like planets and underground in vast caverns, completely hidden from the world above them. Too much water is actually deadly to them."

"So that's why so many human cultures have seen them?" Angie asked.

Ray nodded. "When we first started terraforming planets,

we worked with them to make sure, as best we could, that each planet was suitable for both human and Gray life."

"They didn't need that much space," Tacita said. "Just enough to house a few of what they call their hives."

"They have been expanding with humanities expansion?" Gage asked.

"Yes," Ray nodded. "But early on it became clear that humans were too fearful of the Grays, so the treaty was signed and the Grays have just kept themselves mostly hidden from the human populations on a planet."

"We honestly know very little about them beyond that," Tacita said.

"Have you ever met a Gray?" Benny asked before Gina could.

"Tacita and I negotiated the treaty with them," Ray said.

"We have not talked to a member of their race since," Tacita said.

"With only one exception, no Seeder has talked to a member of their race in any capacity that we know of in millions of years," Ray said.

Silence filled the room and Gina welcomed it as all eight of them sat there, all clearly lost in thought.

So once again, information about the past of the Seeders and humanity had been held from them and now it was suddenly in play. For such a vast universe, it sure seemed to be suddenly damn small.

Gina could feel her anger draining away. Ray and Tacita would have no reason to tell them of the Gray for this mission or for any mission, actually.

"So what do we do now?" Angie asked. "We have about forty thousand long-lived Seeders on *Deep Cycle* that now know about the Grays."

"Not counting our entire command crew," Gina said.

"And since the Grays are losing that fight," Benny said, "they are going to need the help from their mistake to defeat our mistake."

Gina laughed and the others just shook their heads and smiled.

"We will need to talk with the Grays," Tacita said, glancing at Ray.

He nodded. "This is not a secret we can keep any longer among Seeders. We must continue to keep it from the general human populations on planets."

"It seems that Seeders keep a lot of secrets," Gina said. "So that shouldn't be so hard."

"Agreed," Carey said.

The other chairmen nodded.

Gina looked at Benny and he nodded, as if he could read her mind.

She turned to Ray and Tacita. "I would suggest that we move *Star Rain* to the new infestation until we have it contained. *Star Mist* and *Star Fall* can continue to direct the fight in this area."

Ray and Tacita made no move at all, but the other chairmen nodded.

"The aliens are our mess," Benny said. "If the Gray want to continue to help, fine. But they are losing and we need to stop this infestation quickly while it is manageable. We don't have time for million-year-old politics."

"You put our three ships and the six of us in charge of this battle for a reason," Gina said, staring at Ray and Tacita. "Now let us do our jobs."

Ray nodded to that.

Gina watched as Tacita sat dead still, no expression on her face at all.

"The six of us will have you an infestation containment plan in three days," Benny said to Ray and Tacita. "One with the Grays helping and one with the Grays pulling back."

"We will need to talk with the Grays and explain the situation," Ray said.

"I see no reason, since you negotiated the old treaty, why you would not remain the contact person with them," Gage said.

Gina nodded and noticed everyone else did the same.

"*Star Mist*," Angie said into the air, "what are the chances at this point we will defeat the aliens and stop them from spreading through known space?"

"With the forces we have or could bring to bear by a likely foreseeable future point," *Star Mist* said, "the aliens will not be contained. So there is zero percent chance of containment, to answer your question directly."

"Thank you, *Star Mist*," Angie said.

Then Gina watched as Angie turned back to Ray and Tacita.

"You need to do more than explain to them the problem," Angie said. "You need to get them to help us. They live on worlds that will be destroyed by the aliens as well."

Ray nodded. "I do not think the Grays know we are here or where these aliens came from."

"Oh, that's going to be a fun conversation," Benny said.

"Just get them to help," Benny said. "Even it means giving them the technology for the faster trans-tunnel drive."

Ray and Tacita's heads both snapped around to look at Gina and Benny.

Gina was shocked at that reaction.

"Are you saying they only have standard trans-tunnel drive?" Ray asked.

"That's how their ships are moving," Benny said, "from the first reports from *Deep Cycle*."

Ray turned to look at Tacita. She was looking slightly shocked.

Gina had no idea why.

Ray turned back to look at Gina and Benny. "Do not bother with a battle plan where the Grays do not help."

Tacita nodded at that.

Then both of them stood.

"We must consult with a few others who know of and study the Grays," Ray said.

"Please, please," Angie said, "keep us informed on what you find."

Tacita nodded to that. "We will. This secret is now past a point of value."

"And please move *Star Rain* toward the new infestation at highest possible speed," Ray said. "Negotiating with the Grays from a position of power on a huge mother ship will be helpful."

Gina understood that completely.

A moment later Ray and Tacita were gone.

The six of them just sat there.

Finally Benny said, "Well, can't say this job is boring."

Gina could only laugh at that.

CHAPTER 21

Six months later, completely shielded and with a force of eighty military mother ships on board and thousands and thousands of the small attack ships called Sharks, *Star Rain* eased into position near *Deep Cycle.*

Benny had been studying the battle the Grays had been fighting against the aliens and it had become clear that their long-range scanners were not that good. Some alien ships were getting through.

So the chairmen had authorized the Sharks on *Deep Cycle* to take care of the alien ships that had gotten through while staying shielded. That way they didn't give some of those alien ships a six-month free pass.

During that six months, thousands more Gray ships had poured into the area. But the Grays still had no hope of containing this infestation with their slower ships and scanning that wasn't picking up all alien ships.

Ray and Tacita had kept their promise and kept the chairmen informed about what they found from research with those who had more knowledge about the Grays. It seemed that it was always rumored that the Grays had a large region of space and occupied planets in hundreds of thousands of galaxies.

It was also clear that they did not much care for humans, but tolerated them. When on human planets that Seeders had altered and planted human populations, the Grays stayed completely hidden and shielded from the humans and liked it that way.

Benny had suggested that *Star Rain* launch all its ships and *Deep Cycle* do the same and all drop shields at the same time as Ray and Tacita moved to contact the Grays. It would be an impressive show of power and force.

Ray and Tacita both agreed.

It took almost a full day for *Star Rain* and *Deep Cycle* to launch all the ships they had been carrying and spread them out into a formation behind them facing the battle galaxies that would look impressive. The formation covered almost two light years.

And each ship had a destination area planned in the battle and locked in when *Star Rain* gave the go-ahead.

Again Benny was stunned at the scale that Seeders just worked naturally.

Then Ray and Tacita jumped to the Command Center of *Star Rain*.

Everyone in the room bowed slightly when they appeared and dead silence filled the massive space.

It dawned on Benny that his command crew had never had a chance to meet the legendary Chairmen Ray and Tacita. After the last decades, he had forgotten they were special.

Gina stood beside Benny on his right and Ray and Tacita stood beside him to the left.

"Ready?" Benny asked.

Both Ray and Tacita nodded.

"Not a word, folks," Benny said, turning to look at the command crew behind him. "Not even a slight noise. And bow when we bow."

He got nods as he turned back.

"*Star Rain*," Benny said, "Have all ships drop shields on my mark."

"Standing by," *Star Rain* said.

"Now," Benny said.

On one part of the big screen it showed the image of the massive Seeders fleet spread over a large area of space. The military mother ships were slightly in front of their vast numbers of Sharks.

Star Rain led the large fleet and *Deep Cycle* was second and back, showing which ship was in command clearly.

The Gray fleet could now suddenly see the Seeders' fleet. That was going to be a shock, Benny figured.

"Seeders Chairmen Ray and Tacita to talk with the honored Grays fleet commander," Ray said.

Benny knew Ray's words were translated into the language of the Grays and sent to all ships within fifty galaxies. He also knew that the image of the four of them standing and waiting was also being broadcast.

Ray had warned them to not be impatient, that it would take some time for the Grays commander to study the situation and respond. They were a methodical race.

So they all stood, hands behind their backs, staring at the screen in front of them.

It took almost four full minutes before the screen flickered and an image of a Gray appeared. Large head, large round eyes, thin neck and seemingly no clothes at all. Benny had no idea how they told each other apart, since every image Benny had seen of them seemed to be identical.

Ray, Tacita, Benny and Gina all bowed.

And Benny hoped like hell that everyone behind them bowed as well.

"Thank you for speaking with us, Great One," Ray said as he came up out of his bow.

The Gray bowed slightly in response. "It has been many millions of what you call year-cycles since our last conversation. I am honored."

What might have been considered the Gray's mouth did not really move as he spoke.

And clearly they knew Ray and Tacita just fine. And that meant that they either lived as long as Seeders or had a solid hive-mind memory.

"The honor is ours," Ray said. "I would request a private meeting to talk about the situation we face with this dangerous and expanding alien race."

The Gray nodded just slightly. Then said, "It would seem to be in our mutual best interests."

"Thank you," Ray said, nodding.

"I am afraid all of our ships are military in nature and would not be suited for such a meeting," the Gray said. "So this meeting will need to take place in this communication mode if that is acceptable to you, Chairmen Ray and Tacita."

"Acceptable," Ray said, bowing.

Tacita nodded.

"Please take the time you need to prepare," Ray said. "But may I ask permission for our smaller ships to move out around the battle area and help in tracking down and destroying the alien ships while our discussion continues."

The Gray's expression did not change, but Benny would have bet anything it was puzzled.

Ray did not force the Gray to ask, but instead continued onward.

"Our ships are very fast," Ray said. "We can move between galaxies at less time than what we call a day in our time-cycle. And our scanning equipment can pinpoint an alien ship moving throughout this entire battle area from any location."

The Gray seemed to think for a moment, then nodded. "You have our permission. We will talk again in exactly two of your cycle days."

The screen went blank, replaced by the image of the huge battle area.

"*Star Rain*," Benny said, "have everyone scramble to assigned areas at top speed. Let's show the Grays what we can do in the next forty-eight hours."

"And that's exactly what we wanted," Ray said, nodding.

He glanced at Benny and Gina. "Thank you both. We will return before the next meeting."

And with that, Ray and Tacita jumped away.

"Well," Benny said, shaking his head and turning to face his command crew still looking shocked at their stations, "that was fun."

SECTION FIVE

THE PRICE OF HELP

CHAPTER 22

With both the Gray and the Seeders' fleets attacking the new infestation, it had become clear that this battle would be under control fairly quickly.

Gina liked that, like the feeling of actually accomplishing something after so much bad news.

Ray and Tacita had met with the Grays ten times over a period of two months and now, today, back in the conference room on *Star Mist*, they were going to detail out the talks and possible agreement.

Gina and Benny were already in their seats around the large conference table, as were Carey and Matt and Angie and Gage, when Ray and Tacita arrived.

Gina looked for any sign they were tired or happy or anything, but the two just seemed to go through life on a very,

very even level. After being alive for that many millions of years, Gina figured there wasn't that much that could shock them.

After Ray and Tacita were seated, Ray said, "We have come to an agreement with the Grays."

Gina and everyone just nodded.

"The terms are basic," Tacita said. "We will give them the improvements to the trans-tunnel flight in exchange for them sending a large fleet to help us contain this area."

Gina was very happy to hear that their numbers were going to be large enough.

"They will retrofit their military ships with the new drive and build more," Ray said. "They will, with the first fleet of their improved ships take over the defense of the infestation they were fighting."

"Our ships will be free to return at that point," Tacita said. "That timeline should be five years."

Gina nodded to that.

"The Grays believe that in ten years they could have five million of their ships fighting in this area," Ray said.

"Wow," Benny said.

Carey and Gage smiled. Gina felt the same way. Five million more ships plus the million more Seeder ships being built in that period of time will give them a chance at holding the line against the alien ships.

"We have agreed," Tacita said, "to modify our original treaty so that Seeders can know about the Gray, but no human."

"That should protect their millions of cities on human planets," Ray said.

Gina liked that as well until Tacita said the next sentence.

"We must therefore," Tacita said, "remove the human Creators' fleet and the Exterminators' fleet from the fight before the first Gray ship shows up here in three years."

"And how do you intend to do that?" Angie asked a half second before Gina could.

"In six months the mother ship *Evening Tide* is scheduled to arrive here," Ray said. "Chairmen Leigh and Oliver have offered to unload the military ships they are bringing and take both fleets back about halfway to the human occupied sector and find them a suitable planet for a home base."

Gina nodded and the room was silent. Gina knew that *Evening Tide* could hold every ship in both human fleets without a problem.

"And if they don't want to go?" Benny asked.

"That will be up to you and Gina to make sure they agree," Ray said. "We have no choice. The Grays fighting with us on this will make the difference."

Angie laughed. "And you told the Grays who created the aliens, didn't you?"

"We did," Tacita said. "And said they are being dealt with."

"We fight their fight," Ray said, a hint of anger in his voice, "clean up their ancestor's mess, they get to start over and settle down in a galaxy all their own. It is the fairest deal we can offer them."

Gina just shook her head.

"Bad blood still flowing deep after millions of years," Matt said, clearly disgusted.

"We should have just left them in the empty-space bubble," Gage said.

Ray and Tacita said nothing to that.

CHAPTER 23

Benny and Gina stood in front of their command chairs, watching the big screen as *Star Rain* made final approach to The Creators' fleet of ships. The fleet looked tired, even from a distance. It was only a matter of time before they would no longer be able to go on.

He didn't much like the solution that was required for the two human fleets, but it was better than anything he could come up with. And from what they had learned about the two fleets of humans, they had always hoped to find a good place to settle, but had yet to find anything suitable.

And then a few hundred thousand years, they had only fought to contain their ancestor's mistakes. So they had taken no time to look for a new home. With the aliens on the move, no new home would be safe.

But the Seeder scout ships had found a couple of planets in a galaxy about halfway back to human space that were perfect, one for the Creators, one for the Exterminators, and yet close enough the two cultures could work between systems in trade.

And the galaxy could be protected from the aliens.

It was an ideal solution and one he and Gina had to sell. There was no other choice.

With the Grays coming into the fight here, there was a slight chance the aliens could be stopped and defeated. And a slight chance was better than they had had for the last few decades.

"Holding position with The Creators' mother ship, *Stahl*," *Star Rain* said.

Benny glanced at Gina. She took a deep breath and nodded that she was ready.

"Drop shields and ask for a conference with Chairman Havemann," Benny said.

Benny and Gina had decided they needed to do this in person, so they were going to ask permission to go on board the *Stahl* as no one in that fleet could teleport since they were all human.

A moment later, Chairman Havemann appeared on the screen in front of them. Benny was shocked that the younger-looking woman they had met the first time was showing signs of aging and had a pretty good streak of gray in her hair now.

Havemann smiled and nodded. "Wonderful speaking with you again, Chairman," she said bowing slightly. "But I assume since you and your magnificent ship are here, there is a problem."

Benny and Gina both smiled at her and nodded.

"There is," Gina said. "Benny and I would like to ask

permission to talk with you and your command crew in private on your ship if we could."

Havemann nodded, no longer smiling. "Give me fifteen minutes to set it up in a conference room and I will send the location."

"No need," Gina said. "We will just jump to your location when you give the okay."

Havemann shook her head. "You can do that?" Then she laughed and said, "Of course you can do that. Fifteen minutes."

"Thank you, Chairman," Gina said and cut the connection.

Benny shook his head and asked, "*Star Rain*, without your translation, will we be able to talk in person?"

"There has been no translation," *Star Rain* said. "You have been speaking their language when you need to."

Benny laughed and glanced around at the command crew, a few of who were nodding and smiling.

"It felt so normal," Gina said, shaking her head, "I didn't know that either."

Benny laughed. "Never too old to learn I guess."

"How old are you anyway?" Gina asked, smiling at Benny with that sly grin he loved.

He laughed. "Old enough to know better, Chairman."

Then he kissed her.

CHAPTER 24

Gina wasn't surprised at the slightly shabby feel to the conference room when they transported on board the *Stahl*. It had what looked to be old metal panels on the walls that were gray and carpet that looked worn and forgotten.

The table was a fake wood but was actually metal and the chairs were just simply folding chairs of some sort. The air had a faint stale smell to it as well, as if it had been used and recycled a few million times too many.

Chairman Havemann stepped forward and shook both their hands.

Gina had liked Chairman Havemann from the start and liked her even more in person. But Gina was surprised at how tiny Havemann was. If she stood four ten, that would be tall.

And the other two with her were also very, very short. Shorter than Havemann. To the humans, she and Benny must have appeared like giants. Clearly millions of years of hundreds of thousands of generations living on board a ship had made height something that wasn't required.

Havemann wore a dark blouse and dark slacks and no shoes. Her face looked even older in person. Clearly the stress of being the chairman was wearing on her quickly.

The other two also wore dark shirts and slacks and no shoes. Maybe shoes had also become something not needed in shipboard living. Or they were just too much use of resources to be of value. Gina bet it was the latter.

Havemann introduced the two men with her as her first officers, one military, the other construction and operational. Both were older than Havemann looked and both clearly were shocked at the size and height of she and Benny.

One man wore thin glasses and his name was Lenscarry and the other had almost no hair and his name was Shadelost. Gina doubted she would remember who was who, but she would try.

Havemann was her prime concern.

After all introductions were made and the five of them were seated around the table, Havemann started off by asking a question before Gina could say a word.

"You said humans occupied millions of galaxies? How is that possible?"

Gina glanced at Benny and he nodded, clearly telling her she should go ahead and explain some history, something they hadn't done much of with The Creators.

"When your people left human space four million years

ago," Gina said, "humanity was just starting to spread out from its home galaxy."

"Four million years?" Havemann asked, clearly stunned.

"Your people slept for the first million of those years of travel," Gina said. "Then what you called 'the great awakening' happened. But as we said before, you are a far distance from human-occupied space."

"During those millions of years," Benny said, "a group of long-lived humans spread out, seeding on habitable planets the basis of more human societies and helping them reach maturity."

"That's why we are called Seeders," Gina said. "Millions of galaxies are now alive with humanity because we seeded humanity on them."

Havemann nodded, then looked into Gina's eyes and asked simply, "Are we going to be able to rejoin the mass of humanity at any point in the future?"

"That's exactly why we are here," Gina said.

Beside her Benny was nodding.

Havemann sat up straight and glanced at the two men beside her, then back at Gina.

"We believe that you and your people have sacrificed enough in this fight," Gina said. "Our scouts have found a wonderful planet and system for your people and another system and planet for The Exterminators' people. Both in the same empty galaxy."

"How far away?" Havemann asked.

"At your speeds," Gina said, "about one hundred thousand

years. But we can transport your entire fleets of ships in one of our mother ships and have you there within four years."

"Four years?" Havemann said.

Gina nodded. "In the direction of humanities area of known space."

"You can start fresh and build and eventually join all of humanity from there," Benny said.

"Why would you do this for us?" Havemann asked.

"It's what we do," Gina said, hoping Havemann would ask no more.

"We are Seeders," Benny said. "Our entire mission is to help humanity grow and flourish. We will be there to help you as well if you need it and ask for it. Otherwise we will just stay out of your way and invisible."

"And we will protect the outsides of your galaxy from any chance the aliens will get there," Gina said. "But we require one promise in return."

Havemann nodded.

"We require that you will never try to build an alien race again in any fashion."

Havemann looked at Gina for a moment, then just broke out laughing in a high, light laugh.

Beside her the other two were laughing as well.

"That, Chairmen," Havemann said, "after the last few hundred thousand years, will be an easy promise to keep."

CHAPTER 25

Benny and Gina, over the next full year, worked with the humans on both fleets to toss away their bombs and start learning how to build homes and planet dwellings. Benny had no illusion that these two fleets of humans were in for the task of their lives.

And for many generations into the future.

What Benny was the most excited about was in that year, they got the two fleets to agree to work together to learn and build trade agreements between their two cultures. Everyone on all the ships would spend the four years in travel to their new home learning about living on the surface of a planet.

Benny had no doubt that a vast number of them would never be able to leave their ships. But a large percentage would, and that would be enough to start the two cultures.

So everyone on board the two fleets was going to get a crash course over four years while on the mother ship *Evening Tide* in living on a planet and building towns and eventually cities.

And maybe even how to make shoes. Not one person on either fleet wore shoes.

What had pleased Benny over the last year of working with the two fleets was the fact that Chairman Havemann and Chairman Airst of The Exterminator fleet got along great.

Both of them felt that this was a huge gift for their people.

Now, in just a short year, both fleets were docked on board the *Evening Tide*. In just a few hours, the *Evening Tide* would start the journey to take them to their new homes.

Benny found that amazing.

They were sitting across the same conference table in the *Stahl* with Chairman Havemann. The *Stahl* was docked on the large main deck of the *Evening Tide*, something that Chairman Havemann had found amazing.

This final meeting was to basically say goodbye. Benny had no doubt that he or Gina would ever see Havemann again. He liked her. She had courage and intelligence and the ability to think for all her people.

They had talked for a few minutes about the crash education program that was going to be offered in the next four years. Then Havemann looked up at Benny and then at Gina and sat forward.

"Can you tell me something in private?" Havemann asked, her expression suddenly very serious. "I promise to take your answer to my grave."

"That depends," Gina said. "Ask and we will tell you if we know the answer or can tell you or not and why."

Benny nodded.

"What is the real reason behind this sudden desire to help us find a home?" Havemann asked. "We all know the battle against the alien spread is not going well. Why do you want us out of the way? I understand we were not helping much, but we were helping, weren't we?"

Benny laughed and glanced at Gina who smiled.

"Yes, you were helping," Benny said.

Gina said into the air, "*Star Rain*, please ask *Evening Tide* for permission to put a privacy bubble around this room."

"Done," *Star Rain's* voice came back clearly. "Your complete privacy is guaranteed."

"Thank *Evening Tide* for us," Gina said.

"I will," *Star Rain* said.

"Wow," Havemann said, shaking her head.

"Your fleets were helping overall," Gina said. "It was not a method that Seeders condoned or would ever do because we believe in letting a race make their own decisions on a planet."

"Which is why we are stopping their expansion outside of each galaxy," Benny said. "What the aliens do inside the galaxy is their business. We just can't let them expand anymore."

Havemann nodded. "And if stopped, they will die off because expansion is the only thing they know to stay alive."

"Exactly," Gina said.

"So if we were helping," Havemann said, "why pick this point to get us a new home and take us out of the fight my ancestors caused?"

Benny glanced at Gina and then turned back to Havemann. "Because we have better help arriving in a couple of years."

"Better help?" Havemann asked, clearly puzzled.

"At least five million ships to help stop the aliens," Gina said. "And they will all have the new, fast trans-tunnel drives as we do."

"Wow," Havemann said. "That will turn the tide."

"Eventually," Benny said. "Or at least we hope so."

"So who is bringing these ships?" Havemann asked.

"That's the part we can't tell you," Benny said. "Even under a promise of secrecy."

"But they have one requirement for joining the fight," Gina said.

"Let me guess," Havemann said, nodding. "No humans can know about who they are. So it was time to help us find a home."

"A win-win situation is how we looked at it," Benny said. "After millions of years, you finally get a home and out of a war."

"And we get help that might be able to stop the aliens," Gina said.

Benny watched the small chairman nod her head slowly.

"I have to be honest," Havemann said after a few moments, "I doubted we could hold our fleet together much more than a few more generations. So this timing is perfect. A complete win for us."

"Good," Gina said.

"In fact," Havemann said, "the truth is we were discussing asking for your help to pull us out of the fight before you arrived with your offer."

Benny laughed. "Great minds think alike."

"And you know we would have helped if you asked," Gina said.

"I know that now," Havemann said.

She stood and moved around to shake Benny and Gina's hand as they stood as well. "I have to get my people learning how to live on something that isn't metal and flying through space. Going to be a very quick four years."

Benny smiled at the chairman. "I have a hunch you'll get them ready just fine."

"I hope so," Havemann said. "And I hope this fight here goes as well as you plan."

"So do we," Gina said.

With that Benny and Gina transported back to the command center of *Star Rain*.

Two hours later, from their apartment, Benny and Gina watched as *Evening Tide* vanished, taking two amazing fleets of humans to their new homes.

Benny actually felt sad to see them go. And considering how angry he had been at them when they first arrived here all those years ago, that was pretty amazing.

And when he mentioned that to Gina, she just nodded, then said, "I felt like I have just said goodbye to a friend."

"We did," Benny said. "We did."

SECTION SIX

A MUCH, MUCH BIGGER PROBLEM

CHAPTER 26

After the departure of the two human fleets, it took almost five years for the first Gray ships to start arriving. It seemed that they had a few more problems with containing the alien outbreak than they had thought they would have.

Gina hadn't been the slightest bit surprised.

The other scout ships had found no other outbreaks, so now the daily routine had settled into battle reports and meetings with newly arriving chairmen to brief them on the problems they all faced.

The six chairmen had started having dinners together every other week to just informally talk about the problems and compare notes. They switched apartments for each dinner and who did the cooking and Gina had started looking forward to those nights.

They were wonderful breaks every few weeks with friends.

There really were no notes to compare. The battle was still lost and with every passing day, the aliens spread out more and more, a flood that even though they were trying, there seemed to be no way to stop.

Every few months Benny would ask *Star Rain* to calculate the odds of victory against the aliens and every time, without fail, even with the Gray ships pouring into the area, the answer was zero percent.

Now, after ten years and over three million Gray ships and almost a million Seeder ships, that answer from *Star Rain* seemed wrong to Gina. To Gina, it seemed as if containment was starting to happen. But when Benny did his standard question, *Star Rain* said once again zero percent chance of defeating the aliens.

Benny and Gina had just finished going over the daily reports from not only their area of battle, but the other three major areas when Benny asked his question.

"That seems so wrong," Gina said.

Benny shrugged. It had been the same answer so many times, Gina doubted Benny even heard it anymore.

"We need to ask the question in a different fashion," Gina said.

Benny shrugged once again and indicated she should try.

"*Star Rain*," Gina said. "Will the area of battle that we focus on every day ever be contained?"

"Yes," *Star Rain* said.

Benny's head snapped up and he stared at Gina, a total look of shock on his face. She hadn't seen him be this surprised in a very long time.

And she felt exactly the same way.

She chose her words carefully for the next question.

"How long will complete alien containment of this area take?" Gina asked *Star Rain*.

"One hundred percent containment of this battle area will be achieved in approximately six-hundred-and-seven years."

Benny opened his mouth, but Gina stopped him from speaking.

"How long will containment take in the area *Star Mist* focuses on?" Gina asked.

"Fifty years less," *Star Rain* said.

"And the area *Star Fall* focuses on?" Benny asked.

"Approximately the same amount of time as this area," *Star Rain* said.

Benny stood there, his mouth opening and closing as he stared at Gina. Behind them the light chatter of the command center had silenced. Gina could tell that everyone was shocked by these answers.

"Let me ask the next question," Gina said to Benny and he indicated she should go ahead.

"So this entire battle area will be contained and the aliens defeated in this area in just over six hundred years?" Gina asked. "Correct?"

"That is correct," *Star Rain* said. "At the current levels of fighting and technology. More ships or other fighting advances will shorten that time frame by factors."

Benny just shook his head.

"*Star Rain*," Gina said. "When Benny has asked you repeatedly the chance of defeating the aliens, you have always responded with zero percent chance. Please explain."

"There are other alien incursions," *Star Rain* said.

Gina wanted to just sit down on the deck in front of her command chair. She felt sick.

Completely sick.

"You have got to be kidding me," Benny said.

"I am not joking," *Star Rain* said.

"How do you know this information?" Gina asked.

"I had access to the Creators' ancient records," *Star Rain* said, "many of which were not even accessed by those on the Creator ships."

"Oh, no," Benny said, turning and walking away a few steps.

"*Star Rain*," Gina said. "Please explain."

"The Creator's fleet continued movement for thousands and thousands of human generations. Much information was lost in those generations to the humans on board. The aliens were first created and planted just over two-point-one millions years ago and the human ships moved on without stopping to study their project."

"They forgot, didn't they?" Gina said.

"The information on the alien culture was stored and most likely forgotten, yes," *Star Rain* said. "The reason was that the alien growth would have taken dozens of human generations before the aliens would even have built their first ship."

"Ah, the standard impatience of humans," Benny said, shaking his head.

Star Rain went on. "The information and experiment was

discovered again six-hundred-and-ten-thousand years later and the experiment was tried again."

"Let me guess," Benny said, "they did not stick around to see the results and it was forgotten again."

"That appears to be the case," *Star Rain* said. "The third experiment was attempted two-hundred-and-eighty-thousand years ago, leading to this outbreak. The human fleets did not move on this time and realized their mistake and attempted to stop the spread."

"But the first two attempts were never stopped," Gina said.

She just wanted to walk away from all of it. How was this even possible?

"I have no evidence to prove otherwise," *Star Rain* said.

Gina just shook her head. No wonder Benny's question always had the same answer. With two other outbreaks going for far, far longer. *Star Rain* was correct.

They really did have no hope.

Zero percent chance that humanity and Seeders and Grays could be saved.

CHAPTER 27

Benny took a few deep breaths and then glanced at Gina. "We need to show this to the others."

Gina nodded. "And Ray and Tacita."

Benny nodded. *"Star Rain,* would you please ask the chairmen of *Star Mist* and *Star Fall* to join us here in the command center? Also invite Chairmen Ray and Tacita. Tell them it is an emergency."

"They have all agreed," *Star Fall* said after a moment.

Benny glanced back at their command crew, many who were looking very worried. "Everyone listen closely, but do not interrupt."

All the crew nodded as if their heads were pulled by the same cord.

A moment later Carey and Matt appeared, looking worried. Right behind them Angie and Gage, also looking concerned.

"Been a while since an emergency meeting," Gage said.

"About ten years," Benny said, realizing he hadn't missed emergency meetings in the slightest.

"I'd have been happy with another ten," Matt said.

Benny could only agree to that.

"Bad?" Angie asked.

"Very bad," Gina said.

At that moment, Ray and Tacita showed up.

All of them were standing, facing each other in front of the command chair.

Without a word, Benny asked *Star Rain* his standard question that he had been asking for years.

"Zero percent chance," *Star Rain* said.

He noticed that around him everyone but Gina nodded. Clearly they all had been asking the same question of their ships.

"Now," Gina said, "let me ask that same question in a different way."

She asked about containment of their area and the entire area of the three command ships and *Star Rain* said six hundred plus years if there were no more advances in fighting technology. Less if more ships joined the battle or there were advances.

Benny could have heard a pin drop in the back of the massive command center.

Gage shook his head and spoke first. "The two responses do not make sense."

"They do if there are other alien incursions," Benny said. "*Star Rain*, please explain about the Creators' ships as you explained it to us."

After *Star Rain* finished, again intense silence filled the command center.

Ray and Tacita both looked washed out, as if they suddenly had no blood in their faces.

Carey and Matt just stared at each other.

Angie and Gage looked angry.

Benny knew they needed more information to even get moving at all, so he said, "*Star Rain*, please show the path of the Creators' ships after their awakening to this area of space. Illustrate that path with a green line."

All of the chairmen turned toward the big screen as *Star Rain* first put up what looked like a mist-like three-dimensional cloud. Benny knew that each tiny dot of light represented a galaxy or group of galaxies. The scale was impossible to grasp in any real way.

A green line zigzagged through the mist. He knew it had taken The Creators almost three million years to follow that line.

Benny then said, "Please show with a red dot the first alien experiment location."

A red dot appeared back near the point of the start of the green line.

"At normal alien expansion," Benny said, "please show in red all affected galaxies from that experiment."

"This would assume the aliens of the first experiment were identical to the third," *Star Rain* said. "There is evidence in the records of the Creators that they were, but it is not definitive."

"We understand," Benny said. What he didn't want to say was that maybe the first aliens were even more efficient.

A vast part of the cloud turned red.

"*Star Rain,*" Ray said, "would it be possible to adjust the scale of this to also show in green the original human galaxy and the human-settled area of space?"

"Certainly," *Star Rain* said. The scale shifted to take in billions more galaxies and the original human galaxy blinked in green and all human galaxies were in green.

The red line and the green line looked impossibly close together. And the number of red galaxies far, far outnumbered the human ones.

"Oh, no," Tacita said softly.

"*Star Rain*, please estimate how close the aliens are to the human galaxies at standard trans-tunnel speed?" Benny asked, his stomach now twisted down into a tight lump.

"At closest possible incursion with these assumptions," *Star Rain* said, "Approximately eighty thousand years."

Silence.

Finally Benny said, "*Star Rain*, on this same illustration, pinpoint the second Creator experiment and the projected expansion of the aliens."

A second red cloud of galaxies filled the mist and actually overlapped the first. Thankfully that cloud went away from human space, but more than likely toward Gray space. Benny had a hunch they were not going to be happy to hear that.

Benny just stared at the vast wall of red. The area they were fighting right now, that would take them six hundred years to control, was just a small blemish on the larger area.

The scale was impossible.

"*Star Rain*," Ray said, "what is the likelihood that this scenario is a reality?"

"Sixty-one-point-two-three percent," *Star Rain* said.

Benny just shook his head. Way too high, but the only way to be sure was to go look.

And those alien areas were a long ways from where they were now.

A long ways from any Seeder ship, actually.

CHAPTER 28

Gina stood there staring at the huge cloud of red and the small cloud of green. And the Gray controlled area wasn't even marked because no one knew exactly what the Gray area of space was.

But Gina did know the Grays were in this fight completely as well. They had hives on almost every human planet in every galaxy. If the humans were overrun, the Grays would be as well.

Silence around the eight of them filled the command center. It wasn't a good silence. And if the feeling of hopelessness she was feeling became the way of life, they would all be in trouble. Something had to be done and done soon.

"*Star Rain*," Gina said. "How long would it take this ship to get to the edge of that second expansion from here at full speed?"

"Ninety-one years," *Star Rain* said.

"And to the first expansion area?" Benny asked, following her lead.

"Two hundred and ten years, approximately," *Star Rain* said. "Again, using these assumptions."

"We need faster ships," Benny said.

Slight nods.

Benny turned to Ray and Tacita and waited until they both looked away from the image of red and were looking at him. Gina liked it when he did that. It got people, sometimes including her, to pay attention.

"The new drive we have, if my understanding is correct, is a standard trans-tunnel drive with seven other trans-tunnel corridors opened inside it."

"That is correct," Ray said.

"And each tunnel gives us another factor in speed, correct?" Benny asked.

Gina wasn't sure what Benny was asking, but he was pushing for something.

"Yes," Ray said. "It doubles with each new tunnel. Two, four, eight, sixteen, and so on."

"So we need faster ships," Benny said. "We have to go look at that area and find out exactly what is going on and we can't spend hundreds of years doing that before we act in response."

Benny waved at the big map of red and Ray and Tacita both nodded.

"So get those two who invented the new trans-tunnel drive working on more speed," Benny said. "We need to get there in twenty years, not two hundred. Faster if possible."

Again Ray and Tacita nodded.

"The six of us and our crews will spend the next three days running over every bit of data we can dig up from the ancient Creator records and every possible scenario," Gina said.

The other four chairmen were nodding, letting her and Benny take the lead.

"We need you to find out if even more speed is possible and if so, how long would it take to retrofit all three of our ships," Benny said.

"All three?" Tacita asked.

"You put us in charge of this fight here to win it," Benny said. "We are the young ones, remember, the ones who can face unknown situations and deal with them, as we have done here."

"This fight is now in control," Gina said. "You need our crews and our three ships fighting that situation."

She pointed to the big red mass of galaxies.

The other four chairmen were nodding, clearly in agreement.

"Meeting on *Star Mist* in three days?" Benny asked, looking directly at Ray. "Can you have the information about increasing speed by then? We're going to need it and a lot more if we're going to save not only humanity, but Seeders and the Grays."

"We'll have it," Ray said, nodding.

Tacita nodded as well.

Around them, Gina could feel the hopelessness slide away and the new focus starting to grow in their bridge crew and among the other chairmen.

"*Star Rain*," Benny said, "please remove that image. We all have work to do."

A moment later the cloud of red and green vanished and Ray and Tacita vanished with it.

"Meeting this time tomorrow?" Angie asked, glancing at the other chairmen.

Gina nodded, as did the rest of them.

And a moment later the other four were gone.

Benny reached over and took Gina's hand and smiled.

Then the two of them sat down in their command chair and went to work.

SECTION SEVEN

FINALLY, SOME GOOD NEWS

CHAPTER 29

Benny and Gina hadn't slept that much over the last three days. They had spent a vast amount of time in their command chair, digging detail-by-detail through the records that *Star Rain* had retrieved from lost information in the Creators' ships. They had only moved for meals, showers, and a few hours of sleep.

It seems that *Star Rain* had been correct, the Creators had basically tried the same experiment three times in the almost three million years they had been in space. And they had tried no others, of any kind, thankfully.

But the more Benny and Gina dug, the more Benny was convinced that the aliens they had been fighting here were exactly the same as the ones created in the first two experiments. They were rats bred to build a basic space ship and expand into space. Nothing more.

And what Benny found headshaking was all the reasons for

the three experiments. It seemed to always start when one some young scientist or historian dug up the reason they were in space. And that led to the discovery of the "experiment" as it was called.

All three times the pattern had been exactly the same.

And all three times the reasons had been forgotten when the ships moved on and the scientists doing the experiment died off.

The last day before the meeting with Ray and Tacita and the others, Benny and Gina had worked out how the front lines of the first two experiments might be expanding. It was a vast front, but they also had almost eighty thousand years before that front hit human-occupied galaxies. So they had time.

But on the scale that Seeders worked, that was almost no time at all.

Finally, they had *Star Rain* feed their conclusions to the other two ships and stood.

They were both very worried about the coming meeting. But they had a plan, one worked out with the other chairmen. But that plan assumed that Ray and Tacita would report with a possible chance of more speed.

Benny took Gina's hand. "Ready?"

She nodded and a moment later they had jumped to the familiar meeting room of *Star Mist*.

Angie and Gage were already there and seated, as were Carey and Matt.

Benny considered the four chairmen he and Gina's best friends. The years had done that for them, and if the plan was implemented that they had worked out to fight this new battle, the six of them would be together for a very long time.

And that didn't bother Benny in the slightest.

Before anyone could say anything, Ray and Tacita appeared and took their chairs at the end of the large wooden table. Both were dressed as they always dressed, in black silk pants and shirt for Ray, and black silk pantsuit for Tacita.

Benny just watched as they got settled and then Ray looked at each of them for a moment, then said, "The inventors of the faster trans-tunnel drive believe they can increase the speed by three factors safely."

"Wow," Angie said.

Benny sat back, surprised because that was not the answer he had expected.

"For us math challenged," Matt said, "what does that actually mean for the two hundred year travel time to the first possible experiment location?"

Ray nodded. "The ten-year travel time from the local cluster which contains the Milky Way Galaxy to here would take seven months now. The two-hundred-year travel time would take just over two years."

"Wow, just wow," Angie said.

"That sounds great," Benny said, "But why am I expecting a large qualifier."

"Not a large one," Ray said. "They believe they can have the new drive developed and tested safely within ten years. They understand the theory, just never went beyond eight in the first building expansion because that was so much faster than before."

Benny nodded. He had expected that if the answer was positive on the speed issue, it would take time.

"We have already started the work," Ray said. "Scientists from all over known space are moving to help on the project."

"*Star Mist*," Angie said, "with the increased speed suggested by Chairman Ray, how much would that shorten the projected time of containment and victory in this area of this battle?"

"Containment would come within two hundred years if all ships were fitted with the new drive," *Star Mist* said. "Full victory would be within another two hundred years."

"Wow, good news for a change," Gage said, shaking his head.

Benny looked at Ray. "Honest assessment, please. Can the scientists do this?"

"Yes," Ray said without hesitation. "Possibly faster than ten years, but they asked for ten years to make sure the drives were completely safe."

Benny nodded, as did everyone around the table.

Safe was better. They were going to take enough chances as it was without having drive issues.

"Any idea if the conversion would be large?"

"The scientists don't think so," Ray said. "Adjustments mostly, from what they told me."

Benny was happy to hear that as well. That meant that all the small ships, the Sharks, could have the faster speeds quickly as well.

"So until then, we prepare and keep fighting here," Benny said.

"Push on getting this done," Gage said to Ray.

Ray and Tacita nodded.

"It might mean the difference between surviving and not surviving," Tacita said. "We understand that."

She and Ray stood and nodded, then vanished.

"Good news feels so damn strange," Angie said, laughing.

"Don't really know how to react," Carey said, shaking her head.

Benny just nodded. It did feel strange.

But it wasn't for sure yet. And until they actually had ships moving at that promised speed, he would just wait and see.

CHAPTER 30

For the next three years, Ray and Tacita reported monthly on the progress on the new drive. And each time to Gina it seemed promising. In fact, on the last report, the new drive had been tested and it had passed completely without problems.

So that was getting closer and seemingly ahead of schedule.

She and Benny had dropped back into regular routines and the dinners with the other chairmen had become planning sessions for the possible upcoming mission.

Part of the routine was for both of them to spend an hour every morning in the command chair, linked in with *Star Rain*, going over all the updates of the battle. It was during that routine that *Star Rain* informed them that Angie and Gage were asking for them in a meeting on *Star Mist* with Chairman West.

"Tell them we will be right there," Gina said.

They both stood, still holding hands.

"Is it possible after almost twenty years that West has some news for us?" Benny asked.

Gina laughed and shook her head. "Don't get your hopes up."

"Killjoy," Benny said.

"That's not what you said last night," she said, winking at him.

Benny almost blushed and a couple of the command crew behind them chuckled.

A moment later they were standing in the meeting room on *Star Mist*. Angie and Gage were already seated, as were Carey and Matt. Ray and Tacita had just arrived and were taking their chairs and Chairman West sat next to them, smiling.

Gina could tell this wasn't a bad news meeting as she and Benny sat down. The mood in the air was light.

"Go ahead," Chairman West," Angie said.

West's smile got larger, if that was possible.

"We have recently completed final testing on creating large empty-space bubbles and keeping them stable."

"How large?" Gage asked a moment before Gina could.

"Stability can be maintained at just under two hundred light year diameter," West said.

Gina and Benny both sat back with that. They had been hoping twenty years before, when Benny came up with the idea, of managing just twenty or thirty light year diameter, and a hundred seemed like dreaming.

"Wonderful!" Ray said, smiling.

Gina was shocked that even Tacita was smiling at the news. Gina couldn't remember the last time Tacita had smiled. It looked almost wrong, actually.

"We also have figured out a way," West said, "to create an empty-space bubble that will be in motion. Only sub-light speed, but still in motion."

All of them congratulated West, then Benny asked, "So is the testing done? Can we try this on the battlefield?"

West smiled. "That's the next step."

"What is needed?" Gage asked.

"To create a stable bubble of two hundred light years in diameter," West said, "we need to explode enough of the empty-space bubbles within a reasonable distance of the new bubble at the same time. Too many and the new bubble is too big."

"How many smaller bubbles would that be, approximately?" Gina asked.

"A couple thousand," West said. "Easily done with the Shark ships."

Gina nodded. West was right. It would be an easy operation to coordinate.

"So when do you want to build this first one?" Benny asked.

Everyone waited for West to answer.

Gina expected the answer to be in six months or a year. After twenty years of West working on this, that seemed like a logical time frame to her.

"Tomorrow," West said. "That would be perfect."

All Gina could do was just stare at Chairman West's smiling face.

Beside her Benny just laughed with the other chairmen.

Good news was a very, very strange thing to get at times.

CHAPTER 31

For the first test, they had decided on a corridor of alien ships that were pouring from one smaller galaxy and heading toward another larger one.

Most of the alien ships had not reached the new galaxy, but there were millions of alien ships on the way. And all seemed to be moving along a fairly narrow path.

The chairmen had decided that they were going to try to defend that galaxy and so far were succeeding against the early alien ships. But they had little hope of stopping over a million ships per day.

But an empty-space bubble would certainly help a lot.

Benny couldn't believe his crazy idea might actually work. He had basically given up on it after twenty years. And over the last three years his focus had been on the upcoming mission.

So this news felt almost surreal and he was in a complete wait-and-see mode.

Actually, everyone but Chairman West was. And after scanning through West's last few experiments that had been successful, Benny could see why West was excited and positive.

How they had solved the problem of constructing empty-space bubbles was to discover what drew an empty-space bubble to a certain location. They had copied that and then, when a bubble was deflated somewhere nearby, the replacement bubble formed where they had wanted it to form.

Benny and Gina had been standing in front of their command chair, watching the movement of the ships on the big screen of the area around the proposed empty-space bubble.

"*Rescue One* in position," *Star Rain* said.

Benny and Gina had decided to keep *Star Rain* back away from the test area. But *Rescue One* was close, a little closer than Benny would have liked, actually. But he had decided he wasn't going to second-guess West in any fashion.

"Anchor functioning," West said. "All systems green."

The Anchor was the device that would draw the empty space to it when one was deflated nearby. The Anchor was positioned directly in the center of the path of the mass of ships pouring from the nearby galaxy.

Gina turned to their command crew. "Stay alert on this one. I want data from every possible source."

Then she and Benny sat down in their command chair and Benny said to *Star Rain*, "Be prepared to move us to safety if anything threatens this area."

"Understood," *Star Rain* said.

Gina squeezed his hand.

"Chairmen, we are ready," West said.

Benny knew that all six of them were watching, as well as Ray and Tacita. But it was up to him and Gina to give the go-ahead, since this experiment was in their area.

"Do all systems look clear, *Star Rain?*" Benny asked.

"All systems are ready," *Star Rain* said.

"It's a go," Benny said.

He still wasn't believing that after almost twenty years, his crazy idea was being tested.

"Stand ready," West said to the thousand Shark ships near empty-space bubbles.

They waited. Gina squeezed his hand as they watched the image of a thousand Seeder ships in empty space along with almost a thousand white dots indicating existing empty-space bubbles. All other ships and Gray ships had been sent out of the area for the experiment.

"Anchor working at full capacity," West said. "Bubble One Experiment is a go."

Benny knew at that moment *Rescue One* would coordinate all the destruction of the other empty-space bubbles. That had to be done basically simultaneously to make it work.

For a moment it seemed as if the experiment was failing until suddenly the screen showed all of the empty-space bubbles vanishing at the same moment.

And then, a moment later, a large, large area of the screen showed a perfect sphere, shining white.

Benny knew he was holding his breath because this was the key moment. Would the huge empty-space bubble stabilize?

"How large is that?" Gina asked *Star Rain*.

Two hundred and seven light years in diameter," *Star Rain* said.

"Too much?" Benny asked.

"Too early to tell," Gina said.

One of the worries was how to measure the amount of empty space in all the other bubbles and how that would fill in volume this one large bubble. Clearly they had missed by a little in that calculation.

"The new bubble seems to be stable," *Star Rain* said. "The next sixty seconds will be important."

Nothing was coming from Chairman West yet.

Benny tried to force himself to breathe normally.

Rescue One was still in position and Benny could only imagine the intensity they were working on board that ship. This had been a passion for the crew of that ship for twenty years.

The seconds ticked past and Benny and Gina kept getting more and more data flowing in.

But neither one of them, or any of the other chairmen wanted to interrupt the work on *Rescue One* to ask a question.

Benny found being a spectator difficult at best. But with his hand in Gina's, they sat there, trying to breathe and focusing on the data.

Finally, after almost two full minutes, Chairman West said simply to all of them. "The bubble is stable."

"Confirmed," *Star Rain* said.

"Unbelievable," Benny said, standing.

Gina stood and hugged him harder than he remembered being hugged before.

Behind them, the entire command crew was cheering.

After so many years, they all so needed positive news.

And setting up a vast trap for alien ships was about as positive as it got.

Benny just couldn't believe his wild-hair idea had worked.

And he had a hunch his face was going to be sore from the grin, since grins had been few and far between before now.

CHAPTER 32

O ver the next five hours, more and more amazing data poured into *Star Rain* about the first test experiment.

So much that at times Gina couldn't seem to keep up.

The best that could be determined from the wreckage of alien ships in the small empty-space bubbles that were popped, over six thousand alien ships had been destroyed almost instantly. One of the bubbles had had almost two hundred alien ships in it.

And Chairman West had been correct that by suddenly deflating an empty-space bubble, anything inside was completely destroyed.

After five hours, she and Benny took a break for a late lunch or early dinner. Gina couldn't decide what to call it, and then went back to their command chair.

They managed to get about five hours of sleep that night

before a meeting on *Star Mist* with Chairman West and the others.

When they arrived, Gina thought it felt just flat wrong. Everyone was smiling, including Tacita.

They had had so many serious meetings in this room, fun seemed out of place.

But everyone was laughing and joking.

Gina found it infectious, mostly because she felt exactly the same way.

West looked like he hadn't slept at all and Gina doubted he had, but his mood was jubilant, to say the least.

So for the first thirty minutes of the meeting, he gave a solid report on the successes and a few minor problems they had discovered that could be fixed easily.

"And no repercussions when we pop an empty-space bubble this size?" Angie asked.

West shook his head. "A thousand others will form shortly after, but that would be it. Gravity and time forces will just rebalance. Or we could have another nearby Anchor and it would form another large bubble."

"Are we going to test that?" Matt asked.

"We will, yes," West said.

Finally, it was Gage who asked the question both Gina and Benny had talked about last night and both were curious about.

"How fast can we put these large bubbles out there?" Gage asked.

"That will be up to all of you," West said, smiling. "It will totally depend on how many ships you would like to divert to the process."

"Are you saying that is the only limiting factor?" Ray asked, leaning forward.

Gina was surprised by that as well.

West nodded. "The Anchors can be easily mass-produced and a bubble formed in less than two hours of work. So each bubble needs a coordinating ship and as many Sharks as needed to pop enough smaller empty-space bubbles to make the desired size of the larger empty-space bubble."

"It took your ship and about a thousand Sharks yesterday, correct?" Angie asked.

West nodded.

Gina had a hunch they were going to be doing a lot of calculating very soon on how to disperse fleets of ships to this task.

"How close together can these large bubbles be?" Benny asked.

"Safely," West said, "eight-hundred light years apart. We have not tested that, of course, but the math tells us that is the answer."

Gina just glanced at Benny who was shaking his head. She felt the same way. In the distances between galaxies, that was extremely close together.

"So we could put these up around an alien galaxy, basically," Gina said, looking back at West. "On all the major paths alien ships take toward another galaxy?"

West nodded. "Let me show you, if you don't mind if *Star Mist* downloads a few images from *Rescue One*."

"Please," Angie said.

"*Star Mist*," West said, "would you please show the first image I prepared from *Rescue One* of the path of the alien ships from the origin galaxy to the target where we put the large bubble yesterday?"

"I would be glad to," *Star Mist* said.

A moment later an image of two galaxies appeared in the air, one near Ray and Tacita and one near Angie and Gage.

A white sphere floated between them directly in the path of a mass of tiny red dots that were alien ships.

"This second image is a very rough illustration of how the alien ships leave one galaxy toward another," West said.

Gina watched as a cone appeared. At one end it was basically the shape of the origin galaxy and expanding out like a megaphone toward the larger target galaxy.

Gina was amazed. All alien ships already in transit were inside the cone and the large white empty space was square in the middle of the cone and about halfway between the two galaxies.

"Here is what would be needed and would be possible to stop most alien ships in that corridor," West said.

The image changed to show six large white empty-space bubbles staggered behind the first one and offset in such a way that almost no alien ship could escape hitting one of them.

"A couple dozen Sharks could clean up the few ships that make it along the seams," West said, smiling.

The stunned silence filled the room. Gina could hardly breathe. Was this even possible?

Ray and Tacita just sat there, eyes wide, staring at the illustration floating in the air.

Finally Matt asked, "How long did you say it would take to set that all up?"

"Using the fleet we used yesterday," West said, "two days at most."

Again Gina just sat there beside Benny, stunned. She didn't even know what to say.

Two days?

Just two days?

Nothing in the world of Seeders took only two days.

"*Star Mist*," Angie asked, breaking the silence, "how many alien ships, approximately, will leave that galaxy along that corridor?"

"Approximately sixty-four million," *Star Mist* said.

"Let me see if I understand this completely," Ray said, turning to face West. "You are telling me we can stop sixty-four million alien ships with two days work and a dozen or so Sharks watching for those alien ships that miss the bubbles?"

"That's exactly what I am saying," West said, beaming.

Silence.

Then everyone in the room jumped to their feet applauded.

West looked embarrassed, but kept his grin pasted on his face.

Gina couldn't remember feeling this good before, at least not since they had found the alien problem.

Beside Gina, Benny applauded while he shook his head and then laughed.

"What are you laughing about?" Gina asked him.

"It's going to get real crowded in those rattraps," he said.

She liked the sound of that more than she wanted to admit.

CHAPTER 33

Benny and Gina stood in front of their command chair, watching the daily reports pour over the large screen in front of them. Around them, the mood in the command center was light and there was occasional laughter.

In the weeks after the first initial successful construction of a large empty-space bubble, Benny and Gina and the others worked with West to form teams to build new bubbles.

Or rattraps as Benny liked to think of them.

Larger military ships that could hold a thousand Sharks were the anchor ships.

And by the end of three weeks, they had ten fleets of ships placing bubbles.

Ray and Tacita had managed to get the Grays to join in the guard duty of any alien ship missing a bubble. It seemed the

Grays were very impressed at the Seeders' ability to come up with solutions and were more than willing to help.

By the end of six months, most of the Seeders' fleets were involved with building bubbles and the Gray fleets were doing cleanup around the bubbles.

As a test, West and his team had built a large bubble right in the middle of a large number of alien ships, then waited a few weeks and popped it to make sure the result would be as desired.

Benny was happy to learn that the result was better than hoped for. Deflating a large bubble smashed whatever was inside into pieces so small, they were hard to even identify. Basically, everything inside became nothing more than space dust.

And when the test bubble was deflated, a new large bubble formed close by with another Anchor.

So now, at the one-year anniversary after the first bubble had been formed, hundreds of thousands more rattraps were formed, with Seeder fleets creating them at the rate of six hundred per day.

Benny just shook his head when he learned that number. Seeders never did anything at a small scale.

And tonight, on the one-year anniversary of the first bubble, all the chairmen and command crews from all the major ships in this fight were meeting for a large party to honor Chairman West and his fantastic team. The first real party they had had out here.

Benny couldn't believe how much he was looking forward

to the party, and Gina had spent days trying on different dresses, she was that excited as well.

And she had made him promise that he would dance with her no matter how many left feet he claimed to have.

They had earned a party as far as Benny was concerned. They had done the impossible and won this battle.

It would still take years to block all main alien ship corridors, but only years. Not decades or centuries.

And that just made Benny smile. He still wasn't used to thinking in the vast numbers of years that Seeders thought in. He liked here and now and maybe some thought of tomorrow. So this schedule worked for him.

He just wasn't good at thinking about next century.

But now, officially, this battle was won. *Star Rain* had estimated at this rate of construction, the entire alien problem would be contained in ten years and the aliens would cease to exist in this area of space in less than two hundred years.

The larger battle in the other areas would take more time, but now it was possible to stop all the aliens completely.

And when he asked *Star Rain* the percentage of chance of this entire battle throughout all space being won, the answer was now one-hundred-percent.

That was worth a party by anyone's rights.

Gina came over and took his hand and smiled at him. "Ready to go get dressed?"

"I am dressed," he said, smiling at her.

"I mean in the tux I got for you," she said. "I'm dressing up and so are you."

"How many decades have we been together?" he asked. "You ever seen me in a tux?"

"That's going to change tonight," she said, kissing him. "And I'm looking forward to it."

He laughed. She knew he didn't really mind. But he had to pretend to complain.

She took his hand and then turned him so they could face the command crew that had backed them so well for so long.

"Everyone," she said, "time to go get dressed for the party."

"*Star Rain*," Benny said. "Take care of things until we get back."

"I will," *Star Rain* said. "Enjoy your party. You have earned it."

"We have all earned it," Benny said. "And that includes you."

"Thank you," *Star Rain* said after an uncharacteristically long pause. "The honor has been all mine."

USA TODAY BESTSELLING AUTHOR
DEAN WESLEY SMITH
STAR FALL
A SEEDERS UNIVERSE NOVEL

If you enjoyed *Star Rain*, try the next thrilling novel
in the Seeders Universe series, *Star Fall*! What follows
is a sample chapter.

SECTION ONE

LOST

PROLOGUE

Chairman Ray stood beside his wife, Chairman Tacita on the massive bridge of their mother ship, staring at the day's battle reports coming in from hundreds of thousands of light-years of space. Around them the three tiers of stations were all filled with fifty command crew. The noise in the room was low, only a few conversations.

Ray knew they would win this war. He and Tacita both knew that now. It would take a little more time, but they would win.

The fight had gone on now for over three hundred years. It would take another hundred years to mop it all up. A short time in the life of Seeders like them.

Ray's long gray hair hung down his back as he stood staring at the large screen filling one wall that scrolled all the reports. He had on his normal jeans and dress shirt. Tacita had short black hair that seemed to shine and she dressed as she normally did, with dark dress slacks and a silk blouse.

"We can't let this happen again," Tacita said, her voice her normal calm and level tone as she studied the reports.

Ray glanced at his wife, his partner for more hundreds of thousands of years than he wanted to think about. Her short black hair shaped her face, often giving her a stern look he knew didn't usually match her personality. She was still beautiful by any measure. He couldn't imagine living a moment without her.

He stood over six feet tall and didn't really tower over her. They made the perfect couple as far as he was concerned.

"I know we can't," he said. "We can never be caught off guard again by anything going on near human space. Or anywhere in the universe, for that matter."

The alien experiment they had been fighting for the centuries had threatened to overwhelm human space, destroy millions of galaxies full of human life. Only luck and the sheer brilliance of the six chairmen of three ships had saved them.

But now the battle was nearing its end and victory was at hand.

"Do you have any suggestions?" Tacita asked.

"I do," he said. "Please bring up the Starburst image."

The battle map on the big screen in front of them was replaced by what looked like a point of light with lines radiating in three dimensions from it.

"You are going to have to explain this," Tacita said.

"The center point is the Milky Way Galaxy, since that is

where we have major construction facilities to build new ships for the war effort."

She nodded to that.

"Each line represents one massive ship," Ray said, "a combination battle ship and scout ship, but far larger than any of our mother ships."

"How much larger?" Tacita asked.

"Each ship should be able to hold over three million souls," Ray said. "And many thousands of scout ships and battleships."

"And their use?" Tacita asked. "I assume you intend for them to go out along these lines. Where do those lines stop?"

"We give every ship the new trans-tunnel drives and they go out five hundred years before moving over and returning on a new course back."

"Five hundred years at those speeds will take all those ships beyond any edge of space we have been able to see," Tacita said, turning to look at her husband.

He nodded. "We need to know what exists in the universe before something like the aliens finds human space."

He pointed to the starburst illustration on the screen. "All of the known universe and far beyond. And that's how we find out."

CHAPTER 1

Chairman Carey Noack stood beside the large chairmen's chairs in the command center of *Star Fall*. On the massive wall screen in front of her the daily reports were coming in from all the scout ships. She knew that if anything was abnormal, *Star Fall* would report it to her. But she still liked to scan the reports every day. Habit built out of hundreds of years now of doing the same thing.

At least now the reports weren't about war, but about exploring galaxies. She liked this a lot better.

Carey stood not much over five-four, had long brown hair she kept pulled back, and always wore jeans, a light blouse, and tennis shoes. Even though she had lived now for a very long time, she still looked not a day over thirty. And was still in as good of shape as she had been when she met Matt Ladel all those years ago in the dead Earth city of Portland.

Living seemingly forever was a real bonus about being a Seeder.

Around her the other twenty members of the main command crew were all busy working as well. The command center was exactly the same as the old *Star Fall* command center had been, even though the new ship was ten times the size of the older ship.

She was glad she and Matt had decided to keep the command center looking the same on the new ship. Over the centuries she had grown used to the old size of the command center, having the chairmen's chairs down on the lower level in front of the big screen, then a half-circle of stations behind her, up two steps, then another half-circle of stations around the back wall, up two more steps.

It made the big room feel like a college amphitheater she had classes in back at the University of Oregon. The room was big and impressive, sure, yet small enough that the entire command crew could work as a team.

After they had finished the war with the aliens, which had taken them over three hundred years on the original *Star Fall*, Chairman Ray and Chairman Tacita, the founders of the Seeders, had asked her and Matt if they would be interested in having *Star Fall* shifted to a new and much larger ship for an exploration mission.

A mission that might take them a thousand years to complete. But a critical one to make sure the human galaxies were never threatened again as they had been with the alien infestation.

Both she and Matt, her co-chairman and partner for life, had agreed, and when *Star Fall* agreed to move to the newer, bigger ship, everything had been set.

The construction of the new ship had taken almost twenty years. And now, at fifty years into the new mission, Carey still enjoyed the challenge of every day.

She couldn't imagine ever getting tired of it, actually.

They were going to explore beyond the edge of known space.

She was halfway finished with the morning's reports from the thousand scout ships they had out at the moment when Matt appeared at her side. He was sweating and had just come from doing five miles on one of the many tracks on *Star Fall*.

She didn't even glance at the handsome man she was more in love with now than the day she met him. She knew he would be sweaty and his short brown hair would be going in all directions. It seemed to always do that, even when he tried to comb it.

"Don't even think about hugging me," she said without looking away from the reports scanning past on the big screen.

"Would never think of it," he said, laughing.

A couple of other command crew behind them chuckled. It was almost a standing joke that he would show up after exercise in the command center and try to give her a sweaty hug.

"You know you and your team don't stand a chance this year," he said.

She turned and looked at his sweating face and his grin. "Seems to me that your team has lost to my team every year now for six years."

"Seven," one of the command crew said.

"Seven," she said, smiling.

"This is our year," he said, frowning past her at whoever had corrected her.

"I think this year you should just work on finishing," she said, glancing back up at the screen and all the reports, trying not to smile.

He snorted and said nothing. The last two years his teams hadn't even finished the Tip-to-Tip race, although she had to admit they had given it a good try both years.

The Tip-to-Tip race had been Matt's brainchild about twenty years into the new mission. The new *Star Fall* was so massive, holding over three million people, that Matt had thought it would be fun to have a relay race with ten member teams starting at the bow of the ship and running through the entire ship to the stern, then back to the front.

Tip-to-Tip was born.

It wasn't until the two of them, in their apartment one night, working with *Star Fall*, had discovered just how far that race would be.

Both she and Matt were from an Earth with a country called the United States. The length of the new *Star Fall* was from coast-to-coast. Two-thousand, eight-hundred miles from the front to the back of the ship, about four-thousand, five hundred kilometers.

So Tip-to-Tip would be over nine-thousand kilometers. Or about nine-hundred ten-kilometer races, all linked.

Without a break.

Last year the winning team had done the relay race in just under thirty-eight days. Each member had to run or walk ten kilometers before passing the monitored armband to the next team member.

There were ship hangars on *Star Fall* that were larger than some of the old states in the United States. The ship had been built in space to explore for a thousand years with three million men, women, and children. The ship had been built to go beyond any known space and explore along the way as it went.

It was long, shaped in ways like a long bird, and was the size of a decent moon. Its shields were so powerful that on trans-tunnel drive it could plow through a planet and not even notice it had hit something.

So at first, because of the size of *Star Fall*, Matt's idea of a Tip-to-Tip relay race seemed impossible. But the more they thought about it, the more fun it sounded and now it was a major yearly event for the ship.

Also, it would give a lot of the people living on *Star Fall* some reason to exercise.

Last year over eight-hundred teams had signed up. And Carey had to admit the race was grueling and a lot more fun than she had ever imagined it to be.

This year's Tip-to-Tip race started in ten days. And she and her team were ready. They wouldn't win it, but all that mattered to her was beating Matt's team.

Bragging rights for a full year were wonderful.

CHAPTER 2

After his workout, Chairman Matt Ladel climbed out of the shower, finished dressing in his normal dress shirt, jeans, and tennis shoes, and then checked in with the other nine members of his relay team. All of them were feeling healthy and ready to go.

And so was he. And in three team meetings over the last few months, they had a pretty good plan worked out on how they were going to run the race this year. And barring injuries that had happened the last two years, they would make it.

Last year four of the ten of them had been forced to drop out around day twenty. Running a ten-kilometer leg every ten hours could really stress the body. And most teams didn't finish with all ten of their members still running.

But when they lost four team members, Matt and the others found it almost impossible to run a ten-kilometer leg every six hours. They managed to give it a try, but after three more days, they finally had tossed it in.

Matt couldn't remember being that sore or that tired before.

They had still been in the top three hundred teams, since most teams every year drop out much sooner. Last year only one-hundred-and-forty of the eight-hundred-plus teams that started actually finished.

Carey's team had been one of the finishers and he hadn't heard the end of it all year.

He was in their apartment kitchen, working on getting himself a small snack of cheese and crackers when Carey paged him from the command center.

"Matt. Got an issue."

He knew that tone and those words. When Carey said they had an issue, it wasn't something he waited around for.

He popped a piece of cheese in his mouth and jumped to her side in the command center. Every Seeder could teleport, the only way it was possible to get around on a ship this size.

"We have a scout ship missing," she said as he appeared beside her. "*The Bee.*"

He studied the report on the big screen in front of their chair. He knew the chairman of *The Bee*. Chairman Reed, a good man, an experienced chairman.

Reed liked to smile a lot and drink his beer on off hours. For a Seeder, he was stout and solid. In fact, he was known as a superb brewer and a number of the pubs he liked served his beer at times.

The Bee carried almost two thousand in crew and families

and was on a standard one-week mission with a small military ship shadowing it.

All scout ships went out on rotation for one week, then returned for three weeks so the families and such could have some stability on *Star Fall*. In fact, most families stayed home instead of going along on the week-long missions, even though every person or family on a scout ship had a home both on the scout ship and on *Star Fall*.

The mission of a scout ship was to jump ahead of *Star Fall* and scout galaxies along the route for any signs of alien life.

Seeders had discovered that the universe was mostly empty. Only two races had ever developed the technology to go between galaxies. Humans and the Gray, and the Gray had been first.

Seeders were the branch of humanity that lived a long time and seeded human culture in new galaxies. The aliens they had had to fight were a runaway human experiment.

So the mission Matt and Carey and *Star Fall* was on now was to explore outward beyond the edge of the known universe in search of other advanced civilizations, if any existed.

There were now fourteen ships the size of *Star Fall* moving outward in a starburst pattern, exploring. So far, no ship had come across anything more than a few emerging alien races in a galaxy. And sadly, most of those races would never develop far enough to get off their home planet, let alone survive long enough to expand out into their own galaxy.

But Seeders stayed away from even those low-level alien civilizations, making note of them and then never entering the galaxy again. Space was big enough and empty enough to not need to.

Sometimes Matt found it stunning the scale Seeders worked at. The speeds of the scout ships and of *Star Fall* were such that entire galaxies with billions of stars could go past like signposts on a road.

And right now *Star Fall* was only at half speed, allowing the scout ships to fan out in all directions, scan entire galaxies and report back in. Over a thousand scout ships were out at any given time.

But in fifty years now of this mission, they had not had a scout ship go missing.

Matt didn't like the feeling of this at all.

CHAPTER 3

C arey glanced at Matt when he appeared beside her. She let him get his bearings and see the problem, then the two of them moved to their command chairs.

The two chairs were molded together and when in the chairs the two of them could almost be a part of *Star Fall* and absorb so much more data.

Matt took her hand and they sat down. They always held hands when in the chair. It allowed them to feel more in contact with each other as well as *Star Fall*.

The chair formed in around them, a familiar feeling that Carey had grown to love over the centuries.

"*Star Fall*, show us the last images coming in from *The Bee*," Carey said.

In front of their eyes the image appeared as if they were looking at an approaching galaxy from the perspective of *The*

Bee. It seemed like a normal spiral galaxy, small, but nothing unusual. And it had no reading coming from it.

The Bee planned on holding just at the edge and scanning, then if finding no immediate signs of civilization, doing a complete circuit of the outer edge of the galaxy, then if still clear, *The Bee* would make a pass through the galaxy before moving on to the next galaxy in their week-long mission.

Everything looked perfectly normal until suddenly all data and the image simply cut off.

"Star Fall," Matt said, "any sign of failure on *The Bee* in any way."

"No," Star Fall said. *"Up until the instant of cut-off, all systems were functioning in normal ranges."*

"Theories?" Carey asked.

"I have no explanation for this occurrence," Star Fall said.

Carey did not like the sound of that in the slightest.

"Empty space bubble they missed?" Matt asked.

Carey nodded. That would account for such a sudden vanishing, but all empty space bubbles were tracked by all ships carefully and the Seeders had actually used empty space bubbles as a weapon in the war against the aliens.

"No," Star Fall said simply.

Matt glanced at Carey and she turned slightly to look at him. She could tell he was worried, more worried than she had seen him since the early days of the war.

"I assume the military escort ship with *The Bee* recorded the same thing?" Matt asked.

The military escort ship was the *Sinclair*, with Commander

Tulo in charge. Every scout ship had a much smaller military ship shadowing it, usually screened.

"It did," Star Fall said. "Commander Tulo reported the missing ship the moment it happened and took up a standby position near where The Bee vanished."

"We need to stop and bring in all scout ships," Matt said.

Carey nodded. "I agree. And then send a dozen more scout ships with military escorts to surround the galaxy, but not approach."

"Agreed," Matt said.

They both stood.

Carey turned to the command crew, many of them she had worked with for centuries. Worry covered all their faces.

"We're going to a full stop and bring in all scout ships," Carey said.

No one said a word. A couple of them nodded.

Beside her Matt said, "Star Fall, please drop out of trans-tunnel flight."

"Emergency recall all scout ships," Carey said. "Including The Bee. See if they can hear us and we just can't see or hear them."

Carey turned with Matt to watch the main board as the thousand plus scout ships and their military escorts responded to the return call.

Two minutes later all had responded but The Bee.

Carey felt his stomach twisting in a knot.

"How long until all ships are back on board?" Matt asked a fraction of a second before Carey could.

"Three hours," Star Fall said.

Carey turned to Matt. "We need to get this ship and the scout ships returning protected."

Matt nodded.

"*Star Fall*," he said, "tell the second and the fifth military units to launch on emergency status and protect all returning scout ships and this ship against any threat."

Carey knew that would launch over two hundred high-powered military ships with defensive and offensive capabilities. No families on the military ships.

Star Fall had the capabilities of full defense and offense as well, but no point in taking any chances at all with the three million lives that were on board.

Of the three million souls on board *Star Fall*, over eight hundred thousand were military and their families. For thousands of years, Seeders had not really needed a military branch. But since the war it had become a regular part of any Seeder mission and Carey was very glad they had the military with them now.

NEWSLETTER SIGN-UP

Follow Dean on BookBub

Be the first to know!

Just sign up for the Dean Wesley Smith newsletter, and keep up with the latest news, releases and so much more—even the occasional giveaway.
So, what are you waiting for? To sign up go to deanwesleysmith.com.

But wait! There's more. Sign up for the WMG Publishing newsletter, too, and get the latest news and releases from all of the WMG authors and lines, including Kristine Kathryn Rusch, Kristine Grayson, Kris Nelscott, *Pulphouse Fiction Magazine*, *Smith's Monthly*, and so much more.
To sign up go to wmgpublishing.com.

ABOUT THE AUTHOR

Considered one of the most prolific writers working in modern fiction, *USA Today* bestselling writer Dean Wesley Smith published far more than a hundred novels in forty years, and hundreds of short stories across many genres.

At the moment he produces novels in several major series, including the time travel Thunder Mountain novels set in the Old West, the galaxy-spanning Seeders Universe series, the urban fantasy Ghost of a Chance series, a superhero series starring Poker Boy, and a mystery series featuring the retired detectives of the Cold Poker Gang.

His monthly magazine, *Smith's Monthly*, which consists of only his own fiction, premiered in October 2013 and offers readers more than 70,000 words per issue, including a new and original novel every month.

During his career, Dean also wrote a couple dozen *Star Trek* novels, the only two original *Men in Black* novels, Spider-Man and X-Men novels, plus novels set in gaming and television worlds. Writing with his wife Kristine Kathryn Rusch under the name Kathryn Wesley, he wrote the novel for the NBC miniseries The Tenth Kingdom and other books for *Hallmark Hall of Fame* movies.

He wrote novels under dozens of pen names in the worlds of comic books and movies, including novelizations of almost a dozen films, from *The Final Fantasy* to *Steel* to *Rundown*.

Dean also worked as a fiction editor off and on, starting at Pulphouse Publishing, then at *VB Tech Journal*, then Pocket Books, and now at WMG Publishing, where he and Kristine Kathryn Rusch serve as series editors for the acclaimed *Fiction River* anthology series.

For more information about Dean's books and ongoing projects, please visit his website at www.deanwesleysmith.com and sign up for his newsletter.

For more information:
www.deanwesleysmith.com

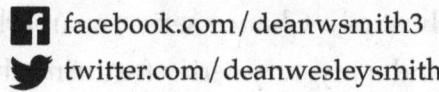 facebook.com/deanwsmith3
twitter.com/deanwesleysmith